THE RUMINATORS

Laura Wacha

Good Riddance Books

With Gratitude

Thanks to Paisley and Viola and Sheila,
who read it,
and to Milo.

Prologue

Frank shook his head at his wife of seventeen years as she stood, back to him, washing the dishes at the kitchen sink. Outside the window the New Mexico sky was dark, and Frank could clearly see his wife's expression reflected in the glass just before she turned to reach for the kitchen towel that was hanging from the handle of the oven door. Once her hands were satisfactorily dry, she faced Frank directly, tilted her head to one side and put both hands firmly on her hips.

"Oh, sure," she said, giving him her familiar knowing smirk.

"Look, Trudy, it wasn't a coyote! Cross my heart. I have never seen an animal like this before..." Frank grabbed the plastic jug from the fridge and poured himself a glass of milk. "I'm a zoologist, fer cryin' out loud!" he asserted, fishing a couple of cookies out of a ceramic pig. "I know wombats, I know echidnas, I know kinkajous, and I certainly know a coyote when I see one. This thing was definitely no coyote!"

"Frank. Dear. Ya know, for someone with a Ph.D. in zoology, you can sometimes be pretty unscientific. Apparently you are an expert on mammals, but I'm an expert on both you and your son and I know one of your wild tales when I hear one. You two are always trying to fool me with your fishy stories." Trudy stuck her fingers playfully in her ears. "La, la, la, I can't hear you!" she said in a singsong voice. Taking her fingers from her ears to put the lid back on the cookie jar, Trudy looked suddenly thoughtful. Maybe she should give her husband the benefit of the doubt. "Okay, Frank, suppose you did see something. It was probably just one of the neighbors' dogs. You know how Shadow used to love feasting on our chickens before we built the new coop. He was probably drooling down memory lane. Lurking about and looking wistfully at our hens, remembering just how good they taste."

Frank dunked his cookie into his glass and looked at his wife. "I don't know, Trudy," he said, "unless Loretta and Carlos have gotten themselves a new pet chupacabra, it wasn't one of theirs..." He managed to get the cookie into his mouth just before it fell apart in the milk and he smiled from the sense of accomplishment. "Plus, whatever it was, it smelled like it had had a recent encounter with a skunk!"

***

The next morning was beautiful, clear and cool. One of those gorgeous autumnal New Mexico days that held a crispness in the air, reminding Frank that winter was on its way and with it the potential for snow. The Mater family lived in the high New Mexico desert at an altitude of over four thousand feet, and although the summers were desert hot, the winters could be mountain cold. Frank glanced up at the sun, already moving into its winter path, and thought it would be the perfect kind of afternoon to climb up on the roof and fix that leak, if there ever was such a thing. Fixing roof leaks was far from being one of Frank's favorite chores, "But if you have to do it," Frank thought, "you couldn't have a nicer day." Frank got out the ladder and began assembling the necessary tools and materials from his workbench out in their small utility building. "Oh darn it!" he swore mildly, "We're out of roofing nails!"

There it was. The requisite trip to the hardware store, no matter what chore Frank choose to tackle. "Well, plenty of time," he sighed, "I'll just let Trudy know I'm going and see if there's anything she needs." Frank looked up at the sky with a beseeching expression. "Please don't have her send me to Walmart..." One of the greatest difficulties of living way out in the country was shopping. No member of the Mater family enjoyed the chore and they were forever running out of something.

The nearest convenience store wasn't what anyone would call particularly convenient. It was over a ten mile drive, clear over on the other side of the Rio Grande, and you couldn't be sure that they would have what you needed or that they would even be open. They might close for anything from a wedding to a softball game. And then you wouldn't be any closer to town. But a simple trip to Belen or Los Lunas for toilet paper could end up being a marathon shopping event for all the necessities of life that would suck up your whole day. Forget it if you needed stuff from Albuquerque. You might as well bring a tent and camp for the night in the mall parking lot.

Setting off in his little maroon Toyota pickup, Frank was happy that today at least he only needed to buy the nails. "And maybe I'll get some more tar paper too," he thought as he bounced down the dirt road towards the interstate. The windows were rolled all the way down and Frank smiled, enjoying the drive in spite of the grit and dust blowing in. As he neared the highway, at the junction where a cattle guard joined the dirt road to the paved one, Frank had to stop short to avoid a white panel van with government plates that barreled by, nearly clipping his front fender. As the van jounced over the bumpy cattle guard, one of its back doors swung open and a canvas sack flew out, landing right near the pickup truck's passenger side. Frank leaned on his horn to alert the driver, but the van continued speeding away, heading down the only paved road on that side of the Bernardo exit. Frank hopped out of the truck, thinking that he'd pick up the sack, follow the van and return the lost item.

The bag was about a yard long, made of dirty white canvas and as Frank approached it he was startled by the smell. The thing stank like the dickens. "May as well see what's inside. I'd hate to go chasing after that van to return a sack of dirty diapers," thought Frank, repulsed. "Phew, it sure does stink like 'em!" He knelt on one knee and gingerly pulled open the string that tied the canvas bag closed and peered inside. "What the heck is that?!" he said aloud. Curled up inside the bag lay a dead animal. But not any kind of animal that Frank had ever seen in a professional capacity, and Frank had seen lots of exotic creatures working as a biologist for the Albuquerque zoo. This creature seemed nearly hairless, just a few coarse black hairs sprouting sparsely from skin of a waxy graphite grey color. Its long snout held sharp teeth that were bared as if in a snarl, and its dead staring eyes were huge, appropriate for seeing in the dark. But the strangest thing about the animal was the row of bony spikes running down its spine as though the creature's very backbone protruded through its skin. It was in fact, Frank thought, the very description of the mythical chupacabra that folk had reported for centuries as coming out at night to drain the blood of livestock.

Although repelled by the horrific odor, Frank leaned in to get a closer look at the creature in the sack. It sure stank like crazy, worse than any dead skunk, but giving off a similarly greasy musky odor. That, in addition to the smell of decomposition. Even so, Frank had to get nearer to make sure that this thing was real. Could this be the creature that he had seen in his yard last night? Was it really a chupacabra? Trudy concluded that the thing he saw skulking around near the chicken coop must have been a neighbor's dog or at most a desperately brave coyote, and although it was tempting to believe Trudy's theory, Frank knew what he saw. And it looked like this thing, just like this thing lying dead in this sack on the road. He grabbed a stick from off of the edge of the dirt road and poked the thing. "Well, it passes the poke it with a stick test," he said. "I declare this creature to be both real, and dead. And real dead, in fact." Frank chuckled to himself, satisfied that he really did see what he thought he saw, and also excited at the possibilities. A chupacabra? For real? He closed the stinky bag and placed it gently in the back of his truck, intending to chase down the guys in the van and find out what they could tell him about the strange sack.

***

The roof never did get fixed. Not that day or any day after.

Trudy would remember Frank asking her if she wanted him to pick up anything in town when he went for the roofing materials. He had sounded as though he intended to come home. But he never did.

Book One - Cousins

1 Philo's Arrival

Shawn gazed glumly out the pickup's rear window at the brown desert landscape going by. His eyes flickered and paused at the tumbleweeds and other wind blown detritus that were stuck here and there in the barbed wire fence. His older sister Marsha sat reading in the front passenger seat, while their mother was at the wheel. Addressing the back of his mother's head, Shawn asked, "Who names a kid Philo anyway?"

Trudy sighed as she glanced at her son in the rearview mirror. "Your Aunt Janice for one. Philo is a perfectly nice name and he's a perfectly nice boy. I know it's been a while, but don't you remember you cousin? You got along great the last time you met."

Shawn rolled his eyes almost audibly. "Yeah, sure we did, but we were practically just out of diapers then! Definitely crayons and play-doh time... You know, conversation was kinda limited..."

Marsha could not resist an opportunity to take a jibe at her younger brother. Without looking up from her novel, she quipped, under her breath, "Conversation is still kind of limited if you ask me, baby brother..." Then, turning briefly to her mother, she asked in her normal tone if cousin Philo had any hobbies. "What does he like to do, this cousin of ours?"

"I'll bet he's a nerd," grunted Shawn.

"Wow," sighed Trudy, "somebody got out of the wrong side of the bunk bed this morning. You'd never guess that it's summer vacation from the way you're grumbling. I'm not sure I can take six more weeks of this!"

"Sorry Mom, I was just looking forward to lots of time alone this summer. I've got stuff planned. Important stuff. Like sleeping late, slobbing around, starting some secret projects. Nothing hard like being polite and sharing a room with some dorky guy I hardly know."

Trudy steered the truck onto the off-ramp that headed for the airport. "I understand, Shawn, really I do, but please let's not judge Philo before you meet him, okay? You might as well get used to the idea of sharing your room for the rest of the summer because Aunt Janice and Uncle Bert need time to get their new business off the ground without worrying about what Philo is up to."

Trudy actually thought it more likely that her sister had sent Philo for a visit to keep them all busy and distracted. Busy enough not to think about what had become of Frank. Shawn and Marsha's dad had been gone for several months now, and his whereabouts were a complete mystery. Months were spent in searching for him, but now that every lead had been followed with zero results, the family was at a loss. Nothing to do but get over the sad cliché of a tragic family story. Dad went to the store and never returned... Trudy glanced back at her son and continued trying to get him excited about his summer roommate. "According to your Aunt Janice, Philo's a quiet kid, but he's smart and full of initiative. Apparently he single-handedly started up a chess club at his school this year!"

A loud groan came from Shawn back in the king cab. "Oh Mom," laughed Marsha, "you just said completely the wrong thing!"

***

"There he is," Trudy said pointing and waving at a lanky kid wearing faded jeans and a t-shirt oddly emblazoned with the

9

slogan "Eat Bagels Now". Recognizing his Aunt and cousins, Philo waved back and walked toward them through the airport's security gate exit. "Hi Philo," stated Trudy, adding in typical Aunt-like fashion, "My how you've grown!"

Philo laughed an easy-going chuckle. "Hi, Aunt Trudy! Yep, that's what happens to us young carbon-based life forms; we grow! Hi Marsha, hi Shane. Long time no nothin'... It's good to see you guys again!"

"Um, it's Shawn," said Shawn, grumpily rolling his eyes again. Marsha witnessed her brother's rude expression and chose to reward him with a nice elbow in the ribs.

Philo pretended not to notice the sibling tussle, and apologized politely for getting his cousin's name wrong. "Oh, of course. Sorry. Shawn." Philo shifted his carryon bag to his other shoulder. "Um, thanks for letting me visit, Aunt Trudy. My folks are really wound up about this new venture. I said I'd help out, but Mom's too nervous, Dad's too calm, and I'd really rather not get in the way. Or in between them, for that matter. That could be dangerous territory and I am just a kid after all!" Philo laughed somewhat nervously and changed the subject by asking, "Okay, which way to the baggage carousel?"

***

After several escalator rides and a short wait, Philo's duffel bag was retrieved from the airline's baggage carousel and stowed in the bed of the Ford pickup. Shawn then opened the passenger door to the pickup, tilted the front seat forward and gestured for his cousin to get in the back of the king cab. "Well, this certainly is interesting," said Philo looking amused. "I've never ridden in a pickup truck before. I didn't know they even had back seats." Folding up his long legs, Philo climbed in. "Why do you suppose it's called a king cab? Not that I'm complaining, but it's not really king-sized, is it?" queried Philo once he was inside.

"I hope he's not going to babble like this all summer," thought Shawn as his third eye roll of the day went unnoticed.

***

All during the forty minute drive south Philo looked excitedly out the window at the passing scenery. It was all so new to the boy from the big city and he gave his relatives a running commentary of all the things he was seeing for the first time. He could hardly contain himself when Trudy pulled the Ford off at the Bernardo exit and crossed the grid in the road put there to keep the cattle from playing in traffic. "Wow, would ya look at that!" he exclaimed, talking about the desert, the mountains, the big blue sky, everything. Trudy couldn't help but smile at Philo's enthusiasm as she drove down the bumpy corduroy dirt road and then down the even bumpier dirt track of their driveway. Suddenly, a roadrunner crossed in front of the pickup and Shawn thought his cousin was going to explode all over the interior. "Wow, did you see that?" Philo exclaimed. "A real live roadrunner!"

"Yeah, meep, meep. Coyote's after you," sang Shawn with a distinct lack of enthusiasm. Trudy shot her son a look that said "be nice", but Philo either didn't notice his cousin's sarcastic tone, or chose to ignore it again.

"So many firsts already and I've only just got here!" exclaimed Philo as he hefted his bag out of the truck's bed. Passing the hummingbird feeder that hung in the yard, Philo paused, grinning, to watch two tiny green birds having an argument and then he proceeded to follow Shawn up the mobile home steps. "I've never been down such a long dirt road or seen so many mountains, or gone inside an actual mobile home! I mean, I've seen these things in movies and read about them in books, but where I come from, the world is paved and flat and people live in apartments. This is all so exotic!"

"Jeez", thought Shawn, "this kid spent the whole drive down from Albuquerque talking... He's never seen a chile ristra, never seen a tumbleweed. Couldn't believe they actually do tumble! For reals! He's never seen cows so skinny; he actually thinks someone should call a vet! He's never touched barbed wire, never seen a volcano, never known such big blue skies. And he thinks the world looks funny without buildings and trees..."

Philo had asked, "Will there be coyotes where you live?"

"Yeah, sure," replied Shawn, "there are so many around our yard! Every night! And they are so brazen that we gotta lock the doors to keep 'em from raiding the fridge!"

Then Philo wanted to know "just exactly how spicy is the food here?" leaving his tongue hanging out for emphasis.

"Not too bad. Just hot enough to melt the cutlery," said a bored sounding Shawn, wondering how a person could even describe the sensation.

"And do kids really get to ride horses to school?" Philo asked, sounding hopeful.

"Oh, Cuz, where'd ya hear that? Only teachers are allowed to ride to school. Just imagine if every kid rode in! There would be too many horses to feed if everyone rode!" frowned Shawn. "Course, they could always feed 'em the leftovers of school lunches..."

Giving his cousin's naïve inquisitiveness a second thought, Shawn said to himself, "Ha, this could actually be fun having Philo around to tease! Fresh blood, so to speak..." Smiling, he led his cousin to the bedroom at the east end of the doublewide. "Well, welcome to New Mexico, dude. This here's my room. You can have the bottom bunk. Throw your stuff over there." Philo quickly took in the mess that surrounded him. Tottering piles of books and magazines, half empty glasses, sandwich sized plates of crumbs, small mountains of Lego bricks. A medium sized mixed breed dog lifted her head out of the mess and gazed calmly up at Philo with sweet brown eyes. "Um, that's Candy, she's a great dog. When she's awake, that is."

"Hi Candy!" said Philo, reaching down to scratch her furry golden head. "Wow, it must be great to have a dog. We can't have one in the city. Or at least that's the excuse Mom uses..." Philo turned his gaze from Candy to the couple of square feet of cleared carpet that Shawn was pointing at just to the dog's right. Putting down his stuff he asked, "Where can I plug in?"

Shawn looked puzzled. "Plug in?"

"Yeah, you know, my laptop."

Trudy popped her head through the doorway. "Oh Shawn, I knew I should have supervised your cleanup efforts... Sorry Philo." Gesturing around the room she said, "I did make some closet space for you, and you can use these two bottom drawers. Have Shawn clean off the desk for your computer." Trudy paused, leaning on the door frame. Frowning at the desk she added," And I don't mean by just sweeping the stuff onto the floor!" Trudy exited before she had fully registered Candy's camouflaged presence in the room. Leaning back in, she addressed her son, "And put that dog outside!"

2 Research

The next morning, Trudy found Philo sitting alone at the Formica kitchen table, drinking a glass of OJ and munching on toast. His face was tilted thoughtfully toward the window, and the curtains were open to the morning sun. "Did you know, Aunt Trudy, that seventy percent of dust is dead skin? The other thirty percent is apparently small particles of soil, some from as far away as Africa. Isn't that amazing? The dead skin dust is apparently transparent, but the dust from soil varies in color according to where it originates. I was just trying to decide if your dust motes are a different color to the dust motes back home."

Trudy looked at Philo with wonder. "Wow, are you always so full of such interesting facts at such an early hour?"

Philo shifted in his chair to face his aunt. "Well, I admit to being a bit excited about being here. I guess I couldn't sleep. I know I said some pretty dumb stuff on the drive down yesterday.

Shawn sure was amused. Anyway, I got up early to do some more research on New Mexico and on this area in particular, and I'm anxious to explore."

"Well, if you're really anxious to explore, Philo, I'll show you where I keep my feather duster!" Trudy paused to smile at her nephew. "Kidding, just kidding..." Trudy went to the coffee maker and removed yesterday's used grounds, dumping them in the bucket of scraps destined for the compost pile. "So what kind of things have you been researching? Your mom said you were a dedicated scholar; what have you discovered?"

Marsha sauntered into the kitchen, shuffling in her fuzzy pink slippers and pushing her brown hair off of her forehead. "Morning Mom, morning Philo, looks like another beautiful day in paradise."

"Yeah, if you don't mind dust!" said Trudy. Marsha gave her mother a quizzical look, but Trudy neglected to clarify her comment about the dust as she switched on the coffee pot. "Philo was just about to tell me what he's been researching about our little piece of paradise. He says that there are some things he'd like to explore."

Marsha sat down on the vinyl upholstered bench opposite Philo and adjusted her nightshirt to cover her knees. She accepted a glass of OJ from her mother and considered her cousin for a moment. He was a rather pleasant looking guy. Wide set blue eyes that gave him a sort of naïve look, sweetly tousled sandy

16

brown hair, plus a couple of freckles in spite of his city-white skin. He'll definitely need SPF 50 at least, she decided. "No offense Philo, but I've lived here my whole life. What could there possibly be to explore? I mean, I know there are some great museums up in Albuquerque, and Petroglyph National Monument is great…"

Marsha paused and looked thoughtful. "Okay, some of the Salinas Pueblo Missions are kind of nearby… and there's the Bosque Del Apache Wildlife Refuge area where there's some great bird watching. The cranes and snow geese that visit there over the winter months are amazing! Oh, and we've got to take Philo to see the Tinkertown Museum! It's this great place just on the other side of the Sandias from Albuquerque. Plus, there's lots of neat stuff to see up north and in Santa Fe… Yeah, okay, I guess I often forget what a great place we live. But most of the sights are pretty far away, Philo; we'd need to do some serious driving and I'm just this close to getting my license." Marsha held up her thumb and forefinger about an inch apart. Trudy reached over and separated them a bit further to show what she thought was a more realistic approximation of when Marsha would be driving.

Philo smiled, appreciative of their easy relationship. He'd been with the family for less than twenty four hours and yet he felt totally comfortable and at ease. "You're right, Marsha," he said, "there is an awful lot of great stuff in New Mexico; I've found all sorts of places on the internet that I'd like to visit. But the stuff I'm really interested in is totally near by. Right around your little burg of Bernardo in fact. You must have noticed that mountain that's practically in your back yard. Ladron Peak, right?"

"Sure, can't miss it! We consider it to be our own personal mountain. When we go out the door, it's what we see to the west. No houses, no roads, just our mountain. But if you're thinking of exploring Ladron, that's some pretty rugged terrain over there, Philo," said Trudy, "lots of lava, granite, cactus and saltbush. Not to mention the mountain lions, bears and rattlesnakes…"

"Aah, but don't forget the gold, Aunt Trudy!" said Philo.

"Is that what you were researching this morning? Prospecting in New Mexico? Well, if you're thinking about prospecting, there's no gold in this area, Philo, just some uranium, silver maybe…."

"Not that kind of gold, Aunt Trudy. I'm not talking about panning for little nuggets! I'm talking about finding the gold bars that were stashed on Ladron Peak after a Wells Fargo stagecoach robbery. This is stuff I discovered before I came to visit. I think I have a solid lead on the gold's whereabouts! Really, I've found a sort of map." Aside from his alert expression, Philo's face was betraying signs of his excitement. His blue eyes were shining and the tips of his ears were turning a bright pink. "Haven't you heard the stories? Don't you know what Ladron means?"

Marsha resisted the urge to giggle at her sweet, naive cousin. "Sure, Philo, ladron means 'thief' in Spanish. The mountain is named Thieves Peak" said Marsha. "According to the stories some Wild West bandidos used the area as a hide out. Probably because of that rough terrain that Mom was talking about. There're lots of stories about gold treasure being hidden up in that mountain, and about people who've gone looking for it. We've all heard local people talk about it. But those same people also say that they've seen flying saucers hovering in formation over Ladron too!"

The kitchen door swung open and a bleary eyed Shawn shuffled in, rubbing at the sleep in his eyes and ignoring the talk of flying saucers. He made a beeline for the cabinet where the dishes were kept, grabbed the biggest bowl, took a spoon from the dish drainer and opened the fridge for the milk. "Uhn," he grunted, noting that the milk was already on the table. He reached up on the shelf for the Frosted Flakes and dumped out the remainder into his bowl. Pouring milk on top, Shawn smiled. He always liked getting the last bowl full, savoring the extra helping of sugar that settled in the bottom of the box. Best way to start the day in his opinion. After two spoonfuls, Shawn looked up, finally registering the presence of his Mom, his sister and his newly reintroduced cousin.

"Morning Shawn," sang Trudy, sounding extra chirpy. Shawn gave a weak smile. "Oh, hi. You guys up already?"

"Yep. Up and learning from Philo where we're going to find our college tuition!" said Marsha.

Shawn gave her a grumpily perplexed look. "You guys aren't talking about scholarships at this hour of the morning, are you? ...Buncha nerds," he grumbled, milk dripping down his chin.

"No fear, brother! Not scholarship applications! No paper work at all. Free gold! Cousin Philo's been telling us about his plan to go looking for the lost gold that's hidden up on Ladron Peak. He thinks he may know where it is. Says he's got a map."

"No way!" said Shawn, waking up a bit. "Ha! Philo, someone is pulling your leg. A buried treasure map? Did you buy it on the internet?" he teased. "Sure hope it didn't set you back much, cause there goes your tuition!" Shawn chuckled, pleased with his joke. "Philo, the lost gold of Ladron Peak can't be real. If there was really any gold up there someone would've found it a long time ago. We've all heard of people searching for it over there, but I'm sure it's just a myth."

"No, really guys! Sure, I've read all of the stories on line, but I'm not just saying this out of left field. I think I may have an actual lead on where the gold is hidden... Not a map, exactly, but a description of where it's hidden." Philo paused to collect his thoughts so that he could tell his story and make his case.

"Okay, listen, this last semester I was doing some research for a paper about train robberies in the old west..."

"So far, so good," interrupted Shawn, smiling.

"Shawn, let him tell it, willya?" said Marsha.

Philo shifted in his seat and leaned forward conspiratorially. "Like I said, I was doing some work on a report for school, when I came upon one particular event that I thought I'd do my paper on. It involved a shipment being delivered to a train station by Wells Fargo, but the stagecoach was robbed before any gold made it onto the train." Philo spoke slowly, choosing his words carefully, so as to convince his listeners he was serious about the gold. "It turned out that one of the guards from that stagecoach had lived in Chicago. Apparently he quit his job after the robbery because he was all freaked out and he moved his family to Illinois. So I checked, did some searching of the guy's family tree, and sure enough, he still had relatives living there."

"Excuse me, Philo, but what was the assignment?" asked Trudy.

"Who cares, Mom, we want to hear about how we can get our hands on some gold, not what Philo learned from writing the report!" complained Shawn.

"It's okay, Aunt Trudy," said Philo, sitting up straight and refilling his glass with juice from the pitcher in front of him. "The assignment was about using source materials, you know, getting as close to the original event as possible. So I looked at old newspaper reports and that's how I found out the guy moved to Chicago." He took a sip of juice and continued. "Anyway, I called up the guard's relatives on the off chance that they knew something about the guy and they turned out to be this lovely doddery old couple. The wife seemed kind of lonely and she loved talking to me about her Grandpa. I couldn't get the old dear off the phone, I mean, she was really sweet... So she mentions some old papers that she might have seen from her grandfather up in her attic, but says she can't climb those steps anymore. She asks me would I come over and help her get some stuff down?"

Philo paused, took another sip of juice and turned to Shawn. "Here's a tip, cousin. Apparently it pays to be kind to the elderly, because I go over to her house and help her get those boxes down from the attic and after some milk and cookies... Whaddya know? It seems that her Grandpa wasn't just the driver of the stagecoach, but he was also one of the robbers too! Apparently he and some other guy set up a fake ambush and then stashed the stuff up in your mountain. Can you beat that?"

Trudy took advantage of the teachable moment. "See, Shawn, the advantages to being dedicated to your studies?" Shawn shot his mother a look but resisted making a comment about the milk and cookies being a so-so reward, as she continued, "But if that's all true, Philo, then surely he must've gone back to where he'd hidden the gold and retrieved it?" said Trudy. "I mean, wouldn't that be the real reason why he would quit his Wells Fargo job and move to Chicago?"

"That's what I thought at first; that he had retrieved the gold and retired to a life of luxury in the big city. But I read everything that I could find in that attic and couldn't find any mention that he had gone back for the gold, or even any record that he had much money. The old woman, his granddaughter, told me that after moving to Chicago he had gotten work at a meat packing plant. What kind of guy would pack meat if he was sitting on a pile of gold?" observed Philo.

"You've got a point, but wait a minute. You said that you found out that this guy also had an accomplice. What about the other guy that was involved? Maybe he went back and took the hidden gold. Stole it from the Wells Fargo guard," said Marsha.

"Hey, you're sharp, cousin! Yeah, I also thought that! Grandpa must have been cheated by his partner. But it turns out that the accomplice was his best bud, he was the second guard on the stagecoach, and, get this, he was shot and killed in the robbery. And I'm pretty sure it was Grandpa that shot him... The old woman told me that she remembered her grandfather being very upset about the death of his partner, often saying in his later years that he 'shouldn't have shot him'. She assumed that he had accidentally shot his friend during the robbery, but I'm not so sure. I found some newspaper clippings, really old and crumbling, and the newspaper account reported that a phantom bandit took off with the loot on a pinto pony after shooting one of the guards."

"Oh, dear, a bit of a sordid tale. This poor old lady's grandfather shot his friend over some gold. But I'm confused. It sounds like you're making some leaps of logic. How do you know your theory is correct? I mean, how do you know that there wasn't a bandit on a pony? Or how do you know that the gold was ever hidden on Ladron? Did you find a map, or what?" asked Shawn.

"Shawn, what do you even know about 'leaps of logic'?" asked Marsha. "Other than that you make them all the time! I think Philo's story sounds worthy of some physical investigation!"

"Thanks for the vote of confidence, Marsha! But yes, I did still think that there were some gaps in my theory. I mean, there could have been a guy on a pinto pony! But then I found, well, not a map exactly, but more of a description of where the gold bars were hidden. Which kind of made the pony-guy story sound like a cover…"

"Jeepers, cuz, what are we waiting for? I'm convinced it's worth a look-see. I give that paper an 'A plus'! Let's go gold hunting!" said a finally wide-awake Shawn.

"Yeah," agreed Marsha, "pack the cooler and start the truck. I'm totally psyched!"

"Not so fast you guys," interjected Trudy, trying to bring the teens back down to earth. "Ladron has some pretty rough hiking terrain! You can't just go gallivanting around over there. Even if I did let you go, and I'm not so sure I would, it would take some preparation. I mean, what are these directions that you claim to have, Philo? Can I see them?"

"Oh, Mom!" said Shawn. "How can you possibly doubt our smarty pants cousin?" Turning to Philo, Shawn said in a stage whisper, "No offense, dude." Then he crossed his arms and looked sulkily down at his empty cereal bowl. "And of course we wouldn't be gallivanting. Since when have I ever gallivanted? Really."

"Not to worry, Mom," said Marsha, pointing to the west. "We'd just be over there…"

3 Over There

It took some convincing for Trudy to let the teens go on an exploratory camping trip to Ladron Peak in search of the hidden gold. They had debated the topic for nearly three days before she finally acquiesced. Philo, Shawn and Marsha put their heads together and came up with many excellent pros to Trudy's meager cons. But somehow, the cons still loomed larger for Trudy, in spite of their smaller number. The kids pointed out that she could easily keep an eye on them with the telescope if she wanted to. And since they could communicate with their long range walkie-talkies, she could keep an ear on them too. Normal cell phone use was spotty at best behind the mesa that separated Bernardo from the interstate, but the view from their front porch across the muddy ditch known as the Rio Puerco to where they would set up camp was totally unobstructed by trees or houses or anything. Trudy would even be able to see their campfire at night with the naked eye.

Still, because the only bridge that went across the Rio Puerco was five miles to the south, and add to that the miles across and then back up north on a terrible dirt road, it was quite a drive from their home over to the foothills of Ladron Peak. "But Mom," said Marsha in her most adult voice, "as the raven flies, it's just a few miles straight west from our front door. We can walk that easy." Trudy refrained from correcting her grammar, holding her tongue and not saying 'easily' although she wanted to, preferring instead to tackle one topic of discontent at a time.

Of course, they would take Candy with them. Candy was a consistently good watch dog, always alert to strangers who inadvertently drove down their dead end dirt road or interloping cattle that came uninvited into their yard and tried to steal her kibble and water. But Candy wasn't a terrifically ferocious canine, not that ferocity would be called for on a simple camping trip.

Another item in the pro column was the fact that Philo was so knowledgeable about the area. Not only was he familiar with the topography (he had downloaded and studied copious quantities of maps), but he had also studied up on the flora and fauna, the geology, and even the paleontological history of the place, like he was preparing for a final exam. And what Philo lacked in practical applied knowledge, Trudy's own two kids made up for, having lived in the area their whole lives. Shawn and Marsha knew how to avoid rattlesnake bites by never sticking your hands or feet anywhere you couldn't see them and they both knew fundamental first aid. The nearest urgent care had always been at least a thirty-five minute car ride away, a long time for a kid in pain when you add in that waiting room time, so Trudy and Frank's kids had learned to be stoic about injuries or illnesses. They knew how to pitch a tent, how to build a campfire and then put it out completely and how to bear proof a campsite. In fact, the brother and sister had been so well trained at outdoor skills because Frank and Trudy had taken them on numerous hiking and camping trips since they were old enough to walk.

Suddenly, the truth hit Trudy like a ton of bricks. There it was, the crux of the matter. The problem wasn't that the kids were going without her, without Trudy, but that they were going without Frank... Without Frank. Trudy shook her head and smiled, banishing the thought, wanting instead to send the message to her children that she trusted them and thought them to be capable human beings. That was her goal. That was what she was bringing them up to be. Trudy finally told the three excited kids that yes, they could go.

***

Although the decision had been made and acted upon, Trudy couldn't help but continue to weigh the wisdom of letting the three kids go on the trip even as she helped lift their tents and cooler out of the truck bed. In spite of Trudy's attempts to hide her motherly concern behind a casual smile, her eldest child could tell. "Aww, Mom, don't worry. By this time on Saturday when you pick us up, we'll be rich!" she said, giving Trudy a big hug goodbye.

"Really, Mom, it'll be fine," said Shawn, trying his best to sound reassuring. "We'll call you on the walkie-talkie as soon as we find the gold. Who knows, maybe we'll only be out here one night and then you can come get us in the morning!"

It was actually Philo who was the most nervous watching the big cloud of dust that followed Trudy's truck as she drove away. It was one thing for him to read about these places, to study the topography from lines on a map, but to actually be out in the wilderness… "What a lot of wide open nothingness," he thought. Philo still had what Shawn called his "city eyes". Being so used to looking at computer screens and book pages, Philo's vision hadn't adjusted to the extreme distances that you could see out in New Mexico. A person could practically see a cow standing just over the border in Arizona if this mountain wasn't in the way. "Well," said Philo as he surveyed the pile of camping gear at his feet. "Where do we start with all this stuff?" He timidly picked up a roll mat. "I haven't been camping since boy scouts. And I quit that in the fifth grade."

"Yeah, Mom told us how you single-handedly started a chess club! A lot more adventurous than the boy scouts I must say!" Shawn was really getting to like his cousin. Philo was so easy going. He didn't seem to mind at all being teased for being such a nerd. He even seemed to tease himself a bit. Philo's positive outlook and slightly self-deprecating tendencies were enjoyable

29

to be around. He didn't get caught up trying to look cool or pretending he knew stuff when he didn't just so that he could fit in. "You know I'm kidding, Philo. I actually think it's kinda cool that you started a chess club. Kinda. About the camping thing - it's customary to start with the tent, but I'm all for eating a small something first," said Shawn, reminding his sister of Winnie the Pooh.

"Surprise, surprise," interjected Marsha, laughing at the image in her head. "Philo, let's you and me walk around a bit while Shawn has a small smackerel and we'll find a good spot away from the road to set up camp. It's not even a remotely busy road, but some ranchers and hunters do use it, especially at the weekend, and we don't want to leave our stuff in plain sight when we go looking for the gold." Marsha shielded her eyes from the sun as it headed slowly toward the horizon. "So tell me about this chess thing. You really go for that?"

Marsha and Philo took off up the slope, leaving Shawn peering into the cooler and Candy turning around in a circle looking for that elusively comfy spot to lie down on. Philo told Marsha about the chess club, saying that it wasn't a big deal, he just liked the game and wanted to play it with guys his own age and not just old men. "I can teach you if you like," he offered.

Marsha cleared her throat. "Well, thanks, I may take you up on it." She paused, weighing her words. "Um, Philo, I've been wondering, if you don't mind my asking, about your name... I don't mean to be rude, but it is unusual. It's Greek right, means

30

'love'? Like philosophy, Philadelphia, bibliophile... Or were you named after someone?"

"No fear, everyone asks. Yeah, it means 'love', and please don't tell Shawn. I couldn't take the kind of ribbing he'd give me on that! But really, Dad picked the name because of Philo Farnsworth. Basically, the guy who invented TV. Farnsworth came up with the idea for how to transmit television images when he was a thirteen year old kid living on a farm. Apparently he was looking at a field that was plowed in rows and got the idea for something called an 'image dissector'. You know, how TV is transmitted in lines."

"Well, not really, but I'll take your word for it," Marsha replied. "So Farnsworth was a smart kid. I guess it tells a bit of what your parents had in mind for you."

"Not quite. What my Dad really liked most about the guy was that after he pretty much invented television, he was disappointed with the results. Apparently Mr. Farnsworth thought TV was all a load of garbage. At least until he saw the lunar landing in 1969. That for him made it all worthwhile. So I guess Dad chose the name because the guy wasn't just smart, but he was principled and thoughtful too... that, and Mom wanted something that ended in the letter 'O'."

"Funny," said Marsha. "Our mom gave Shawn and me names with the letters 'S' and 'H' in them. Do you think that means she wanted us to be quiet? You know, like, shhhh..."

***

That evening, after they had set up the tents and tried out the long range walkie-talkie by letting Trudy know they were okay, the three teens lounged around a small campfire sharing a dinner of roasted hot dogs and tortilla chips and talking about their strategy for the morning.

"We'll want to get an early start; before it gets too hot out," Marsha commented.

"Yeah, I'd kind of noticed it does that here, doesn't it? And it seems to be getting rather chilly now that the sun is going down," noted Philo.

"You have hit on one of the great topics of boring adult conversation here in New Mexico. The weather!" laughed Marsha. "The extremes can be crazy during this time of year. The hours between noon and four can be a bit rough. We'll definitely have to remember our hats and water bottles for sure if we'll be venturing far from camp. And remember to take a bowl for Candy, too. Shawn, did you remember to bring Candy's back pack?"

"I can't wait to see that!" said Philo. "A back pack on a dog." He let out a small snort of a laugh and then looked thoughtful as he munched on a tortilla chip, imagining Candy wearing her pack before switching gears and focussing on tomorrow morning's task. "According to the description from the papers I found, we already covered a good deal of the way to the hiding spot when your Mom drove us here. It must have been a really arduous trip when he was hiding the gold. He told Wells Fargo that a man on a pony rode off with it, but I think in truth he hid the stagecoach and horses in the Rio Grande bosque and hiked over from there. That's about fifteen miles, isn't it? And back then there weren't any roads or even cow paths to follow. I suppose you can see Ladron Peak from the Rio Grande?"

"You can see it all right, but the elevation over there makes the mountain look much closer than it really is. A funny sort of optical illusion. He must have thought he could hike it easily, poor guy," said Marsha.

Philo, lying on top of his sleeping bag in front of the campfire, shifted onto his other elbow to address Marsha. "By the way, what is a bosque, anyhow?" he asked.

"I thought you said you researched this," piped in Shawn, voice muffled from deep within his sleeping bag.

"And I thought you had fallen asleep, Shawn," said his sister.

"I'm awake enough to know when *our* genius cousin needs some assistance from *his* genius cousin!" joked Shawn, sitting up in his sleeping bag and resembling a caterpillar. He then spoke in a voice that he thought sounded professorial. "My dear young Philo, bosque in Spanish means forest, but a bosque around these parts generally means what you city-folk would probably call a wooded area growing by a river." Changing back to his regular voice, he continued, "You know, a bunch of

33

trees. In the flood plain. Here in New Mexico that basically means cottonwood trees. But we've got a lot of issues here about native plants disappearing from flood plains that are being encroached on. Because so many dams get built that change the normal seasonal water flow patterns and because all these nonnative plant species get introduced that take over and kinda mess stuff up. You've seen the salt cedars that are down by the Rio Puerco, right? Those trees with the dark green floppy needle-like leaves? They originally came from Eurasia and were planted to prevent soil erosion. Turns out they are major water suckers and have been pushing out the cottonwood trees ever since. The cottonwoods are those trees with the rustling little heart shaped leaves. They need to be flooded in order to propagate properly, to make more cottonwoods."

"Wow, Shawn, you really have been paying attention to the world beyond the Wii. It seems you're bringing out the conscientious scholar in my little brother, Philo!"

"Hey, I go to school, Sis!" said Shawn in a falsely indignant tone.

Just then a coyote let out a loud yip and wail. The teens listened quietly, appreciating the wild lonely sound. "Cool," said Philo, "that coyote sounded really close!"

Hackles up but body still down, Candy lifted her head from its resting place on her paws and responded with her own version of a howl. Candy often tried, but never quite managed, to imitate the sound. Shawn opened his eyes wide, their whites gleaming in the firelight. "That would be cool, Philo, if that was a coyote. But that sounded to me like the wail of a chupacabra!" whispered Shawn in a spooky voice.

Philo responded with the awed tone that Shawn had hoped for. "A chupa-what?" he whispered back.

"A chupacabra!" hissed Marsha. "Surely you came across them in all your research about New Mexico?" She resisted the temptation to giggle. Of course she knew of the mythological creature, and she also knew that Shawn had developed a taste for trying to fool their wonderfully trusting cousin from Chicago. For some strange reason, Marsha decided that she'd play along, just for fun.

Philo looked at Marsha's face, lit up by the firelight, and saw an oddly amused expression there that made him suspicious. He wisely decided to call the siblings' bluff. "Okay, I'll bite. What's a chupacabra?"

"You'll bite, that's funny!" Shawn laughed. "Cause what a chupacabra really does is suck. Blood! It's this weird animal, really elusive, that sucks all the blood and bodily fluids of goats. Other livestock too, but primarily goats. Terribly vicious creature; it just drains its prey, sucks it dry, and leaves the empty skin and bones. Yuck-o!"

Marsha wasn't much good at Shawn's game and she couldn't stand trying to make her cousin uncomfortable. "Oh don't let

Shawn freak you out, Philo. It's true, there are stories of such a creature. The story goes that chupacabras originated in Puerto Rico, I think, but somehow they came up here from South America. The name chupacabra is Spanish for goat-sucker. Supposedly it's a sort of hairless hunchbacked thing with spines up its back and lots of long pointy teeth." Marsha made a silly face, sticking out her top teeth to resemble fangs. "But don't worry Philo. Contrary to what Shawn says, whenever any chupacabras are found, they turn out to be dogs or coyotes that have some nasty skin disease. You know, mange or something that causes their fur to fall out. They're always dead, always creepy looking, but never actually chupacabras."

"Nah, listen, you guys, Marsha only doubts their existence because she's scared! You don't have any evidence that they don't exist, and if that was one that we just heard, this would be the perfect time for them to be out and about." said Shawn.

"Why, Shawn, because of the full moon? You're getting your mythical creatures mixed up! Chupacabras are not werewolves!" scoffed Marsha.

"No, not exactly because of the moon, but you're close. It's nearly the summer solstice, isn't it? The longest day of the year? And therefore, the shortest night! The chupas are of course nocturnal. They'll be getting more desperate as the nights grow shorter! Less time to hunt." Changing to a fake vampire accent, Shawn added, "Less time to suck your blood!"

Marsha and Philo laughed in appreciation and the three teens got ready for bed by dousing the fire completely and crawling into their tents. While Philo and Shawn dragged their sleeping bags into one tent, Marsha and Candy crawled into the other. As Marsha snuggled down into her sleeping bag with Candy at her feet, they again heard the lonely sounding yips and wails of the coyotes. Candy tried once more to howl and Marsha could hear her brother talking through the thin fabric of the tents. "Hear that, Philo? Chupacabra for sure. But don't worry, you're not a goat." Shawn paused and added, "Are you?" Marsha could then hear her quiet studious cousin give Shawn what sounded like a pretty forceful slug in the ribs.

4 The Rumble

The sun rose bright and early, but the three campers and their dog did a little bit of impromptu sleeping in. When the kids finally awoke, the sun was already warming the high desert. "Aww nuts," said Marsha, reaching in her electric pink back pack for her toothbrush. "We've missed the cool part of the day!"

As Shawn sat on a small granite boulder, munching on an apple and filling his day pack with the necessary snacks he said, "Hey, I am the cool part of your day, every day!"

Philo laughed, looking at his most recently downloaded topo map and checking it against his compass just to be doubly sure of his bearings. Marsha brushed her teeth, using water from a bottle to rinse with and spitting the results behind a four-winged saltbush. "Okay", she said running her tongue over her clean teeth, "I'm ready to go when you guys are. I really thought that sleeping in those bright yellow tents would wake us up as soon as the sun rose. Ah well, let's hope it's not just early birds who get worms." She gave a grimace, thinking of getting worms. "Shawn, have you packed quite enough snacks?"

"Hey, I want to make sure we've got enough strength not just to find the gold, but to carry it out of here too. Gold's heavy, right? You know what I always say. Be prepared!"

"You never were much of a boy scout until it came to the roots and berries lessons. Did you know, Philo, that Shawn can find something to eat no matter where he happens to find himself? City or country. Whether there's a 7-Eleven near by or not! No kidding, I've seen him scrape lichen off a rock in the Sandia Mountains when he was hungry enough!"

"Oh come on, you guys are always having me on. I know I'm gullible, but I'm also pretty knowledgeable too. I know that lichen is that curly little fungus that grows on rocks and trees. I've personally seen lots of different varieties and colors of the stuff, from grey to orange. But really, lichen has got to be inedible."

"No, Marsha speaks the truth; there are some edible lichens. Most grow pretty far up north, but some grow as far south as the Rocky Mountains. I'm pretty sure it was in Colorado that I spotted some and tasted it, not in the mountains near Albuquerque. And, I might add, it was super yuck." Shawn made a face, remembering how bad it tasted. "Truly only for desperate times, which is exactly why my pack is full of Cheetos!"

"Okay, Scoutmaster Shawn," chuckled Marsha, "just make sure you pack some chow and water for Candy in her panniers. Let's get a move on; the day won't be getting any cooler you know."

"Panniers? Are those the backpacks for dogs? You guys are too funny," mused Philo.

"Well, technically they're side packs for dogs. Kind of like the saddle bags they use on horses but of a lightweight material. Heck, I'm not carrying her food and water, she's got two whole legs more than me!" joked Shawn. Candy obediently stood still while Shawn buckled her panniers on. She accepted their weight gladly and in fact loved the sight of them; always an indication of some adventure to come.

Philo informed his cousins that they'd be heading straight west, going up the slope. The teens didn't get the early start they had hoped for, still, it was not terribly warm yet as they picked their way over scruffy sage brush and lumps of rough lava rocks. They were walking in silence for about fifteen minutes when Philo spotted a large horned toad sunning itself on a flat rock. He had almost stepped on the spiny prehistoric looking lizard before he noticed that it was a living thing and not just part of the rock. "Willya look at this!" he exclaimed. "What a beautiful creature!"

"Wow, and it's a whopper!" said Marsha. "I've always been fond of horned toads. Of course, it's not really a toad you know, which is fairly obvious just by looking at the thing. Sorry, Marsha stating the obvious..."

"But, interesting factoid alert! Did you know," interrupted Shawn, "that some species of horned toad are able to squirt blood from the corner of their eyes?"

"Trust you to know something as disgusting as that!" frowned Marsha.

"It's not disgusting, it's called 'auto hemorrhaging' and it's apparently pretty effective at thwarting predators," said Shawn. "Gives them a sampling of just how horrible a horned toad would taste."

"Perhaps they taste better braised with a lichen gravy and a side of Brussels sprouts?" joked Marsha in an exaggerated French chef accent.

The horned toad seemed to consider Marsha for a moment, and the look on its face said that it had heard just about enough silliness for one morning. Or more than likely it had merely warmed its cold blood sufficiently to give them a wide mouthed grimace and climb away to safety under a rock. The trio turned back to the task at hand and began trudging once again up the slope. "Ya know," said Marsha, "I don't really much care if we even find any gold. It's plenty nice just getting out of the house and going camping. We haven't done anything like this since

Dad, like, ya know..." Marsha's voice trailed off. She and Shawn hadn't talked about their father's disappearance for some time. Marsha didn't think that she was consciously avoiding the topic, but it made them both so sad to talk about it together, as if it hurt twice as much when they shared each other's loss.

***

The three teens had only been walking for about half an hour, silently skirting around the small scratchy shrubs that grew up the side of the mountain and climbing over lava rocks and granite boulders that were increasing in size. Still, the sun had already reached its pinnacle in the sky, beating down on the teens' heads and making the air increasingly warm. It was nearly the summer solstice, that day of the year when the sun stuck around the longest and it seemed not to be moving at all, but was just hanging there in the sky as though it was an early and permanent noon. The cousins hadn't spoken much, preferring to enjoy the sounds of nothing: the breeze, the beating wings of a hawk flying by and the dog panting along at their heels. Naturally, Shawn was the first to break the silence with a suggestion to snack. Pulling his day pack off of his shoulders and dragging it behind him on the ground he said, "What do you say we pull up a rock, take a load off and eat some lunch?"

From what Philo had gleaned from the old man's notes, he reasoned that they should be getting close to the area where the unscrupulous stagecoach guard had stashed the gold. "Well," he said, "the gold should be around here, if it's anywhere. I think we should sit down and have something to eat. I guess I neglected breakfast. And then maybe we should fan out a bit and scope out the area."

"Sounds like a plan," said Marsha, sitting down on a rock and relieving the dog of her panniers. Candy found a shady spot under a four-winged saltbush and lapped gratefully at the dish of water Marsha offered her.

Within moments they were all resting quietly, munching on sandwiches, sipping water, and listening to the sound of Candy crunching her kibble. Shawn beckoned to his sister to pass the bag that contained the oranges when a low rumble emitted from beneath them. It wasn't just a sound, but a feeling as well. A sort of unsettling shaking kind of feeling, as though the ground was not as solid as it seemed. A few small rocks tumbled down the hill side past them along with the fruit that Shawn had requested from Marsha.

"What was that?" Shawn stated flatly.

"Wow, I knew you guys had earthquakes here, but I never expected to feel one!" said a surprised Philo, hands extended out on either side as if to steady the ground beneath him.

"Neither did I!" said Marsha. "I mean, we almost never have earthquakes that you can actually feel! Usually we hear about them on the news after the fact. We had better call Mom and see if every thing's okay. I mean, was that even an earthquake?

They do a lot of weapons testing around New Mexico, maybe some kind of bomb went off or maybe there was an explosion somewhere?"

"We would certainly be able to see any kind of explosion from up here. We've got quite the view. I mean, we'd see the smoke, wouldn't we? It had to have been an earthquake!" reasoned Shawn.

Looking up the hillside in the direction that the rocks had tumbled down from, Philo gave out a loud whoop. "Well, whatever it was, I think it might just have uncovered Granddad's hiding spot! I spy, with my little eye, something gold and shiny up the hill! Yahoo!"

Forgetting all about the earthquake, and all about contacting Trudy on the walkie-talkie, Philo trotted up the hill to see whatever it was that was glimmering in the high solstice sun. His cousins followed quickly along, as did Candy, not that she cared for gold, but like most dogs was happy to join in on any adventure. As they neared the spot where he had seen the golden shimmer, Philo was sure that what he was seeing couldn't possibly be anything other than the lost Wells Fargo treasure. He shouted back excitedly to Shawn and Marsha who were upon his heels in no time. "This is it! We've done it! We've found the lost..." Philo's last words were swallowed up by a loud crash of rumbles, creaks and rushing wind as the earth beneath their feet gave way and they were all swallowed up by Ladron Peak.

***

Stunned and laying on what felt like a pile of gravel, Shawn opened his eyes and saw nothing but darkness. "Wha- wha- what the heck just happened?" Slowly his eyes adjusted to the darkness around him. Where was he? And where were Philo and Marsha and Candy? Shawn reached out his hands in an effort to push himself up to a sitting position and touched the fabric of what turned out to be Marsha's sleeve. "Hey, Marsha, you okay? Marsha?"

Marsha groaned and sat up, rubbing her eyes at the darkness, and feeling the back of her head for the lump that must certainly be growing there. "What happened, Shawn? Where are we? Is Philo here? Candy!" she called. "Caaandee!" The dog responded instantly, happily bounding up and licking Marsha's left cheek. "Candy, find Philo. Philo! Where are you? Phi-loo!" Marsha's calls were greeted by an echo of Philo's name repeated what seemed like without end.

"What in the world happened? One minute we were right behind Philo, next minute..." Shawn pulled some gravel from his hair and tossed it into the darkness. The sound of the gravel hitting something soft greeted them, along with an "Ow!" from their cousin.

"Philo! Oh, thank goodness you're all right!" said Marsha, breathing a sigh of relief.

"Well, I think I'm in one piece, but can you get Candy off my chest so I can take inventory of my body parts? I know I've still got my face cause I can feel dog slobber running down it!"

"Candy, get off Philo!" called Marsha. Candy obliged by coming over to Marsha and leaning on her. Marsha was glad of the furry comfort, because she was beginning to feel increasingly nervous. "Okay, we're all here, but just where is here exactly? It seemed like the ground just opened up and swallowed us. A result of the earthquake do you suppose?"

"Maybe, but what I'd like to know is if the earth opened up and we fell in, then why is it so dark? Shouldn't we be able to see the hole that we fell into? I mean, it's not pitch black like that time we visited Carlsbad Caverns and the tour guide turned off the lights for a second. Now, that was total darkness. I do see some light, so there must be an opening somewhere, but where? I definitely would like to get out of here. It's giving me the ultimate creeps!" stated Shawn.

"Shawn, try calling Mom on the walkie-talkie," suggested Marsha.

"Great idea, Sis. That is, if I had the thing. It wasn't particularly comfy, so I took it off my belt and laid it next to my backpack when we sat down."

"Terrific." Marsha thought a moment. "Philo, do you happen to have that little flashlight on you?"

"Oh yeah, duh. I totally spaced it. I guess I wasn't expecting to need the thing in the daytime, but yeah, I think I've got it here somewhere…" Philo searched the pockets of his cargo pants until he felt the tiny flashlight. A small click echoed in the darkness as Philo switched it on. It wasn't very bright, but bright enough to let them see that they were in what appeared to be a cave about the size of a small garage but with a high ceiling. "You're right Shawn. I don't see any opening up there at all." Philo winced when what he did see above their heads registered in his brain. "Ack! Guys, you're gonna hate me. What I do see up there is a solid rock ceiling with lots of veins of iron pyrite running through it!"

"Iron pyrite!? You mean fool's gold? We've been sucked underground running after fool's gold?" said Marsha in a shrill voice.

"Oh guys, look, I'm really sorry. I could have sworn I'd seen the Wells Fargo gold. I can't believe I got so excited over iron pyrite. What an idiot." Marsha and Shawn could see Philo hang his head in shame and sorrow.

"Hey, Philo, don't knock yourself out. We came out on this trip to have an adventure. And that's what we're having. Right, Sis?" said Shawn nudging Marsha gently in the ribs, "Right?"

"Yeah, sure, sure. Don't worry Philo. We'll get out. We got in, right? And we'll get out." said Marsha, wishing she were just a little bit more certain.

47

Philo sat searching his brain for an explanation as to how he'd put them all in this predicament. "Ya know, I've heard that iron pyrite can cause cave-ins. It's a mineral and it grows in cracks in rock and apparently it can eventually break the host rocks apart. I'll bet that what caused us to fall through," said Philo.

"No offense, cousin, but I'm not really in the mood for any factoids at the moment. All I want is to see some blue sky," said Marsha.

"Hey, what's with Candy?" said Shawn. Now that they could see each other with the help of the little flashlight, they could see that Candy was staring towards a depression in the wall of the cave. "Turn off the light a sec." Philo obliged and Shawn continued. "Look. That's where the light is coming from. It's dim, but I think it's a tunnel or something. Maybe we somehow fell down into this cave through there and that's our exit. No, wait, that doesn't make sense..."

Philo turned the light back on and moved closer to where Candy was standing. "Well, there doesn't appear to be anywhere else to go. I mean it's lighter down there and we need to get out of here somehow. Let's travel, cousins!"

Philo, Shawn and Marsha all stood up and dusted the sand and gravel from their hair and clothes. Philo's tiny flashlight didn't do much to calm their fears as they all three gazed into the passageway. There was some light coming from out of the tunnel, but not enough to bring to mind the blue cloudless skies they had just minutes ago left behind. "Well, you first, cuz," said Shawn, "you've got the glow stick."

The hole was shaped like a large roughly-drawn oval and was just big enough for them to stand up in, if they didn't use what Trudy would call good posture. Taking a deep breath, Philo took a step, but Candy beat him to it as she charged ahead, tail wagging. "At least Candy thinks it's safe!" said Marsha.

"Of course it's safe, Marsha, it's the way out, why wouldn't it be safe?" said Shawn, laughing nervously.

"Well, for one thing," noted Marsha, "this tunnel, if that's what it is, appears to be sloping downwards and not going up. I mean, I'm assuming Ladron Peak is still above us, right? The world hasn't gone topsy-turvy?"

Philo and Shawn stopped in their tracks. "Oh my gosh, you're right, it is going down."

5 Socorro

Trudy shook her head as she spoke into the phone. "No, the kids are off camping. I don't have to pick them up until Saturday. I'll leave the two-way with the neighbors in case they need anything. I'm sure they'll be just fine, and I'll be back long before then anyway." She tucked the phone on her shoulder as she got her over night case down from the closet. "Look, don't worry! If you need me, you need me..." She replaced the receiver back into the recharging base and undid the zipper on the bag. Frank's mom wanted her to come, and that was that. She had to go. Since Frank's disappearance his mom had gotten sort of needy. It was understandable; Trudy sometimes felt that way too. But Trudy had the kids to think of, so she feigned being a tower of strength for their sakes. She inhaled deeply, a sigh really, the kind of sigh that was intended to cover up a yawn. She was tired, no denying it, but best not to stop and think about it or she worried that she might not have the energy to get going again.

"Finish packing, atta girl, drive to Socorro, atta girl, prop up SaraJane, come back, pick up the kids from their camping trip…" She smiled as a silly thought struck her. "Oh, but Trudy, then you'll all be rich with the gold bars they find and you can all jet off to somewhere wet and warm with palm trees and hammocks and those cocktails with the tiny umbrellas…" Trudy glanced over her shoulder, suddenly feeling goofy for talking out loud before she remembered that she was all alone in an empty house. She zipped up her bag and placed it next to the front door with an odd feeling of finality about the motion, like she was zipping her silly island fantasy inside with her toothbrush. Making the rounds of the house, she checked that the coffee maker was unplugged, that the lights were all off and that the toilet wasn't needlessly running on. Then she exited, bag in hand, and locked the door behind her. "My life is a long list of lists" she said, as the latch clicked into place.

***

Miguel got out of the truck with the Socorro County seal decal stuck on the door and grabbed the snare from the tool box in the back. He checked his belt for his citrus spray and taser, wondering if he should get out the cattle prod instead. "I can't believe they'd just send one guy out on a bear call," he said to himself. "Dang budget cuts." It hadn't been an even remotely dry spring this year, with plenty of snow pack to run off and supply the plants and animals up in the mountains. "There shouldn't even be any reason for a bear to come down here. Probably just a big black stray dog as usual. It is weird, though, all these reports of missing pets and dead livestock. Could be a cat, I guess, a mountain lion or bobcat? Bears generally go for what's in garbage cans, not for what's in family pets." He walked down the wash to the stand of cottonwoods where some folks out for a walk had reported sighting the bear. Miguel shaded his eyes and looked up into the trees, seeing nothing. He walked on down the wash a bit farther, towards another large cottonwood tree, wondering why Animal Control would even bother to send an officer out this far from city limits anyway.

The spot was popular with people who liked to walk their dogs in the evening, but Miguel thought that it wasn't really close enough to town to worry about. "I mean, wild animals have rights too. Or at least they should. Even bears gotta live somewhere. Don't they?" Scanning the sandy bottom of the wash for the big telltale paw prints and seeing nothing but dog and sneaker prints, Miguel walked around to the far side of the big cottonwood. The ground near the tree was littered with beer and soda cans. "Dang kids..." Miguel thought, looking at the mess. "Parties are great. Who doesn't like to party? But can't they clean up after themselves?"

Miguel walked back to the truck to grab a garbage bag so he could do his good deed for the day. "May as well call in while I'm here," he thought. Picking up the radio's handset, he tuned to the correct frequency and called for Carla to come in.

"Hey Miguel, are you having any luck? Did you sight that bear?"

"Nope, nothing out here. No sign of anything. Not unless the bear's been sitting in the shade having a cold one. This place is littered with cans. But the only bear is the one growling in my stomach. Look, I'm gonna head back to town and get some lunch."

"Sounds good. Then head back into the office. I've got some paperwork for you!" laughed Carla in a singsong voice.

"Oh joy. See ya soon." Trash bag in hand, Miguel headed back to the trees to pick up the litter. As he approached, an oddly shaped animal crept up into the small group of cottonwoods. "Hey, there is some critter here!" With the sun in his eyes, Miguel could only make out a silhouette, but it looked nothing like a bear. It did have a sort of humped back, with broad shoulders something like a bear would have, but this creature was thin with long legs and what looked like a thin tail. "Maybe a mountain lion?" was Miguel's first puzzled thought, "But maybe more canine in shape?" Miguel approached cautiously, curious, but chiding himself for leaving the snare back at the truck. "Well, I'll just get a look at it and see if I can see what it is and see what kind of equipment I'll need."

***

Trudy pulled the pickup into her mother-in-law's gravel driveway and sighed. "I sure do wish I'd gone camping with the kids," she thought. "Now why in the world didn't I?" She switched off the engine but remained in the cab, having half a mind to turn the key again, put the truck in reverse, and go straight to the Smith's for some groceries, ice, and a cooler, so that she could drive out to Ladron and join in the hunt for gold. What fun the kids must be having!

"Too late," she muttered aloud to herself. For there, silhouette visible in the screen door of the cinderblock bungalow, stood SaraJane, watching and waiting for her daughter-in-law to arrive. Trudy sat in the quiet of the truck wishing she didn't have to get out. But this was late June in central New Mexico and the vehicle's interior was already heating up. The screen door of the house opened with a squeak and out came a worried looking woman in her late sixties. She was trim, dressed in neat jeans and a flowered blouse and wearing her grey hair short like Trudy had always known her to. She definitely didn't look helpless, and hadn't ever asked for anyone's help until Frank's disappearance.

Trudy quickly put on her chipper face and got out of the cab of the truck and waved hello. "SaraJane, so nice to see you! I'm glad you called, I was feeling lonely without the kids." These weren't exactly truths, but for SaraJane's sake Trudy resorted to the white lies. Trudy did genuinely like Frank's mother, but seeing her always brought Trudy's thoughts back to Frank and his inexplicable disappearance. And she wasn't exactly lonely without the kids. Trudy always had too many tasks and chores to do to be lonely. In fact, keeping busy was Trudy's main objective these days; keeping busy so as not to miss Frank. But now here she was, missing him all over again and wondering what made him take off. If that's what happened. It was a well worn path for her brain to travel down

The typical story, a Saturday morning, the father of the family goes out to the store to pick something up and never returns. Unlike the classic pack of cigarettes or gallon of milk, Frank had gone to the hardware store for some supplies to fix the perpetually leaking roof. There were loads of hardware and home improvement stores in a fifty mile radius and no reports of him at any of them. Plus nothing appeared on the credit card bill that day or since and no one had seen his little truck. Frank had simply vanished. Trudy shook her head to try and shake the old mystery loose and told herself that he was simply fed up with fixing stuff and he left, even though she would never really believe it.

"Oh Trudy, I'm so glad you're here! Chi-Chi is missing! You've got to help me find him! Help me make some posters. I've called the animal control. They say lots of pets in the area have gone missing, a whole spate of them. They've been getting twice the usual volume of calls. There must be a ring of chihuahua thieves!"

"Oh dear, poor little Chi-Chi. Don't worry SaraJane, I'll help you find him. It's not the first time he's taken off. I tell you, you need to get him fixed!" scolded Trudy. "He has a chip doesn't he?"

"Yes, yes, I know, I know, I promise, I'll get the poor dear fixed if we find him. Maybe breed him one more time? If he comes back, if we find him." SaraJane had always had chihuahua dogs since moving to New Mexico from New Jersey as a young bride. Her beau had gotten a job at the Tech College in Socorro right out of university and they had married and and moved to this very bungalow that they were standing in the driveway of. One of the first things SaraJane did, even before furnishing the little house was to buy a chihuahua puppy. She told her husband that it was necessary if they were ever going to fit in. She had loved chihuahuas ever since. Trudy, a native of New Mexico, could take the tiny yappers or leave them, preferring more substantial cross breeds like Candy. Far less needy and you never had to worry about losing them.

They entered the house which was nice and cool in spite of the heat outside. "I see you got the swamp cooler fixed," commented Trudy.

SaraJane headed straight for the kitchen table where she had her computer set up. "Yes, yes, needed a new pump. I got Ramon from next door to do it for me. He's a dear. Here, Trudy, there's a jpeg of Chi-Chi that you can use for the poster on my desktop. I know you're so good at that sort of thing. Would you like a sandwich or some coffee and banana bread?"

Trudy had studied graphic design as an under grad and now did freelance work, putting together web sites, designing logos, creating pamphlets. "Sure, SaraJane, a sandwich would be great. It shouldn't take me but a few minutes to make some posters and them we can walk around the neighborhood and put them up and look for Chi-Chi. So what do you want the poster to say? When and where did you last see Chi-Chi?"

SaraJane stood at the counter, her back to Trudy as she filled the coffee maker with water. "Just say he disappeared from this neighborhood on the morning of June 20th..."

"Are you serious?" interrupted Trudy. "He only just went missing this morning?" As soon as the words came out of her mouth, Trudy felt awful. Of course Frank's mother would be touchy about the disappearance of someone she loved, even if it was just a dog. "Oh, SaraJane, I didn't mean it to sound like that. I just thought he'd been gone longer. I'll make these posters and we'll go out. I'm sorry."

Her apology was interrupted by the ringing of the phone. SaraJane looked hurt as she went to answer it, but her look changed to pure joy as she spoke into the receiver. "Yes, I'll be right there." Hanging up the phone and turning to Trudy it was obvious from the changes in SaraJane's face and posture that the little dog had been found.

6 Underground

"Okay, this doesn't make sense. Maybe we should go back. This tunnel, or passageway, heck, it looks like a hallway almost, it isn't leading us to where we fell in. It's only going down and away. Down, down, down!" Marsha scratched her head not so much as a gesture to facilitate thought, but in order to remove more sand and gravel from her scalp.

"You're right, Marsha, it does look like a hallway. The walls are pretty doggone smooth and straight. But look, the light is getting brighter! Must be the way out," observed Shawn, choosing to ignore Marsha's comment about their downward direction.

"Well, I imagine that we've fallen into an unused mine. That makes some sort of sense, doesn't it? The tunnel we're in certainly does look man-made." Philo stopped and put his hands on his hips. "Are there any old mines in this area? Your mom mentioned silver and uranium..."

58

"Probably an iron pyrite mine!" joked Shawn, making his sister wince at the comment.

Sometimes Marsha thought that her brother tried too hard to be funny, always making with the jokes. She was also beginning to think that her cousin tried too hard to find the reason behind every event. Who cared what kind of mine they were in? "Guys, can we focus on getting out of here? We can worry about how we got in later. Much later."

"Aww jeez," Shawn said. "Let's stop a minute. I'm tired and hungry. All I can think of is the half a sandwich I left sitting on a rock up there. I'll bet there's a real happy raven having at it right now."

"Yeah, let's do that. Stop a minute. Sit down. Think. Make some sense of the situation. We've been walking a while, or at least it seems like a long time... It's still getting lighter in this direction, but what if our exit is back where we came from?" questioned Philo.

The teens all sat down, leaning their backs on the rock wall of the tunnel. Marsha beckoned to Candy. "C'mere dawg. You are behaving like this is some fun adventure we're on, but I'm kind of scared." She circled her arms around the dog's head and addressed the boys. "This tunnel hasn't gone up, not even one tiny degree. What if we missed something in that first cave we were in? What if we get lost? Hey, what if the flashlight batteries give out? And what if...?" Marsha didn't finish her thought, thinking instead that it was best not to get all panicky in front of the guys.

Shawn couldn't help but detect the mounting discomfort in his sister's voice. "Whoa, Marsha, chill! We're okay, we're all in one piece. It's still lighter up ahead than it is behind us and Philo's flashlight is one of those wind-up kind. Haven't you heard the whirring?" said Shawn in his most laid-back voice.

Marsha stood up quickly, startling Candy, with her hands balled up into tight fists. She couldn't stand it when Shawn tried to get all reasonable with her. "Yikes, sorry, yeah sure Shawn, I guess I'm just not too happy about being trapped UNDERGROUND!" Instantly feeling stupid for exploding, she reached out again for the dog and patted her head.

"Marsha, sit down, breathe. Like your brother said, we're gonna be just fine. We'll all get out soon, not a doubt in my mind. And no, I don't know why this tunnel is refusing to go up, but we haven't really been walking all that long, it just feels like it 'cause we don't know where we're going," reassured Philo. "Plus, we couldn't possibly get lost, we can always go back..." He wanted to add, "and dig," but thought better of it.

Marsha sat down again with them all in a row along the path, backs leaning comfortably, legs bent at the knees. "All right, guys. I'm sorry." She gave a nervous laugh. "Mom always says that Shawn and I take turns being alarmists. We never get worked up about the same thing. That's a good thing, I guess. I must admit that this is gonna be a pretty great story to tell when we get outa here."

"Are you kidding? Mom would never let us go anywhere ever again if she knew we were trapped in an old mine! And you're really close to getting your full driving permit! You can't breathe a word of this!" Shawn smiled at Marsha.

"Shawn, it's not like it's our fault or anything. We didn't cause the cave in. The ground just swallowed us whole!" said Philo. "Aunt Trudy couldn't fault us for that."

"I don't care," said Marsha, drawing small circles in the sandy floor with her index finger, "tell Mom, don't tell Mom, just as long as the ground that swallowed us alive spits us out in the same condition, I'll be okay with it." She managed a weak laugh. "Hey, all this worrying's making me thirsty; anybody got any water?" Philo uncapped the water bottle that he still had slung around his body and passed it to Marsha. "Aah, thank goodness for Philo's amazing utility belt! You are like Batman crossed with a boy scout."

She brushed the sand from her hands, took a sip and passed the bottle to Shawn who did likewise and passed it back to Philo. Pouring the last bit into his open palm, Philo called to Candy. "Hey, where's Candy? Candee!" he called. "She must have gone ahead... Hey Marsha. You call her, she listens to you."

Marsha called the dog's name, hearing it echo from both ways along the tunnel. "That's odd. She's not coming. Philo, shine the light this way." Philo obliged, shining the light at the sandy ground as Marsha indicated. "Well, I see her paw prints going off ahead. Let's go look for her."

The three got up, dusted off their pants and headed off in the direction of the mild glow ahead. Philo held his flashlight low, keeping it shining on the path. The ground continued to be sandy and Philo could clearly see the dog's prints. He wanted to make sure that she was heading forward and hadn't somehow doubled back. "Hey guys, um, look at this, willya?" Philo stood still, winding his flashlight and shining the beam onto the floor of the tunnel.

"What the…" sputtered Shawn as he looked at where Philo's light was shining on the path. Although the light was dim, the impressions made by feet other than Candy's could plainly be seen. They weren't the shoe prints of humans, of that they could be sure. Nor were they made by the paws of a dog. "Yikes, I've never seen a print like that before. What in the world could have made that?" wondered a stunned Philo. "It looks, well, um, jeez, I don't know what that looks like."

"A chupacabra!" exclaimed Shawn.

"Oh, don't be such a dope, brother! Remember? Chupacabras are mythical? That means made-up." Marsha turned her attention from the strange prints that she couldn't comprehend to the whereabouts of the dog she loved. "Hey, we better find Candy," she remarked. "Caan-dee!"

The kids ran along the path, Shawn in the lead, until Philo grabbed him by the neck of his t-shirt and hissed the words "Stop. Wait. Slow down. Look, there may be some creature up ahead. Some wild animal. Sure if we run and make a lot of noise we might scare it off, but it's possible that we might back it into a corner and cause it to fight! I don't know what made these prints or whether or not it's carnivorous, but I think we should at least proceed quietly. I mean, look at them. To me they look, um, ape like!"

"Ah, so not the dreaded chupacabra," Shawn whispered, "it's the dreaded Bigfoot!"

"Shawn, you can be such an idiot! Don't you know when to stop with the jokes? Philo's right, let's slow down and quiet down. I mean, I'm worried about Candy, but stop. Listen, do you hear anything?" said Marsha.

Shawn looked hurt and muttered quietly, "It could be Bigfoot..."

Philo and Marsha both said, "Shhh" in unison, and after a moment all was silent. Marsha put her finger to her lips and cupped her hand around her ear. "Listen," she whispered faintly. Up ahead a very small pinging noise could be heard, like the drip of a faucet in another part of the house into an enamel sink. "Do you hear it? It sounds like tapping. Tip, tap. Taptap tip. It's not a regular sound, like a drip, I mean, it's not a repetitious pattern of tapping. What could be making that sound?"

Philo began walking quietly down the tunnel and motioned for the siblings to come along behind him. More cautiously this time, straining their ears to hear, the teens walked along the sandy floor of the passageway, pausing every now and again to check for footprints. The strange noises continued to get louder, tapping out of rhythm, tap tip taptap tip-tap, until they were accompanied by what sounded like a mumbling sort of noise. The tunnel began to look even more manmade, with the walls becoming increasingly smooth and square, until suddenly, they came upon a junction. There were ancient looking timbers framing the entrances of the two different tunnels that were before them and both seemed to have an equally bright glow emitting from them. The cousins stood still, looking blankly at the options.

Turning to Marsha and Shawn, Philo whispered, "Which way?" with a shrug of his shoulders, when out of one of the tunnels came Candy, tongue hanging out and tail merrily wagging behind her.

"Well, there you are!" said a newly relaxed Marsha, "You silly dawg, you had us all worried." She got down on one knee to give the dog a happy hug and a scratch behind the ears. "Come on, girl, you haven't been mauled by a chupacabra or a Sasquatch, have you? You know what's ahead, dontcha? That's right; show us the way, Candy."

Shawn raised his eyebrows at his sister's new found sense of humor. Glad that she was feeling better, he joined Marsha and Philo as they followed Candy who happily trotted in the lead. Their spirits had definitely been lifted by the return of the dog and by the continued increase in intensity of the glow up ahead.

"Oh wow, this must be a mine we're in. And I think it's still operational. I mean, willya look at this? We've come to an actual hallway!" said a smiling Marsha, pointing at some timbers framing the ceiling.

A more sober Philo commented "Yeah, but these footprints are still really weird."

"Maybe the miners use pack animals to get out whatever they're mining instead of vehicles. So what? Let's go, I want out! I want what's left of my sandwich!" said Shawn, passing the others and hurrying ahead. The tunnel, pathway, hallway, whatever it was, was getting brighter and brighter so that Shawn was able to see in front of him for some distance without the help of Philo's light. He could tell that the light was even stronger up ahead and he ran, the sound of his feet muffled by the sandy floor, expecting to somehow end up outside, in the fresh air, even though the path had still been heading down.

Suddenly the passageway ended, emptying Shawn into a larger room where several people appeared to be working. He stumbled slightly, but quickly recovered his footing, and looked up at what he assumed were a group of some sort of miners.

Totally relieved and somewhat out of breath, Shawn exclaimed, "Oh thank goodness, we've found people!" But his relief quickly turned to confusion and then shock when he realized that the miners, the workers digging with picks at the walls of the cave, weren't people after all. Shawn took in the scene before him, but he couldn't process it. Couldn't quite believe his eyes…

7 The Miners

"Thanks for the sandwich, SaraJane. I'm so glad you've got your Chi-Chi back," said Trudy as she put her purse on her shoulder. "It's awful about all the pets that the Animal Control said were missing or found dead. I sure am glad that whatever is attacking the cats and dogs of Socorro didn't get your little guy." Trudy had almost called Chi-Chi a little morsel, but managed to restrain herself.

SaraJane spoke to her chihuahua in a babyish voice. "Yes, he's my little schnookums, isn't he? Aren't you glad to be back with your Mamma?" Then, looking Trudy in the eyes she promised she would get Chi-Chi fixed a.s.a.p. to stop his wandering. "Look Trudy, thanks so much for coming. You don't need to go back, though. Why don't you stay the night? We'll order in. Pizza Hut or something. Just us girls, no kids. And little Chi-Chi of course."

"No, SaraJane, thanks and all, but I think I actually might go and find the kids' campsite and bring them some food. I sort of miss them and I'll bet they're running out of s'mores supplies by now!" she added with a grin. She adjusted her purse on her shoulder and headed for the door. "Bye-bye Chi-Chi, be a good little chihuahua!" she said, as she climbed into her truck and started the engine. Waving goodbye, she backed out of the driveway then turned left at the main road. She decided against the grocery store, opting instead for a quicker stop at the Mini-Mart where she topped-up the gas tank and purchased some of Shawn and Marsha's favorite snacks. She would just have to guess at what kind of food Philo liked, but as he was a teenager, anything sweet or salty or fatty would likely do. She also bought a couple of gallons of water, a bag of ice and a cheap Styrofoam cooler to put it all in. Securing the supplies in the truck's bed with a bungee cord, she climbed back in the cab and headed north toward the Interstate.

***

Shawn looked around at the underground cave. The space was lit by lanterns placed on rocks around the chamber and Shawn could see seven or eight figures before him, small people each with a pick ax or some other tool in hand. Shawn felt for a moment like he had stumbled into the diamond mine belonging to Snow White's little friends. "No, wait," Shawn thought, "these aren't the seven dwarves. These miners aren't even human!"

68

"All fours!" shouted a strange sounding voice, just seconds before Marsha, Philo and Candy came out of the passage and joined Shawn in the open space. The three cousins stood and stared at what appeared to be a small herd of wide eyed goats that were standing and staring right back at them. Candy looked up at Marsha, then calmly approached the nearest goat and licked its face, like it was an old friend.

"Well, whaddya know?" said Philo, relaxing. "Underground goats! This trip to visit my favorite cousins has certainly been full of surprises. Goats in a mine... Ha, Shawn, no monsters, no cryptids, just some stout little goats!" Philo smiled and shook his head, relieved at the comic turn of events. "Well, they got themselves down here somehow, so I'm sure we'll be able to get out too."

"No, wait Philo, I'm sure I saw, I mean, they were holding pickaxes, they were..." stammered a confused Shawn. "Guys, these goats! They were standing up. I mean on two legs! And they were holding tools! Using pick axes and shovels. Guys, these goats didn't just wander into the mine, they are the miners."

"Ha, enough, Shawn, you gotta let it go! Your big-city cuz won't swallow every daft story you you try to peddle..." As the small group of goats in the room gazed with their weird goat eyes at the humans, the small black and brown goat standing next to Candy gave a bleat, and they all began to assemble themselves into what appeared to be a line with

Candy at the rear. In ant-like formation, the goats began to trot out of the large chamber into another passage way hewn out of the rock wall. The teens were left alone, mouths hanging open, looking around the small cave. There were a number of lanterns standing on flat rocks giving off ample light, and lying on the sandy floor, as if some phantom workers had simply lain them down and vanished, were several pick axes. Leaning near the tunnel that the goats had gone down was a short handled shovel, and scattered about the chamber were some canvas buckets that had been fashioned into small saddlebags. Some of them contained chunks of what appeared to be natural rock salt crystals.

"Okay, so what just happened?" said a perplexed Marsha. "Am I crazy or did that one goat get all the other goats to line up and leave? And Candy with them? I gotta sit down, this day is getting weirder and weirder!"

"All right," said Philo, trying to be reasonable as always. "We stayed up too late last night. I know I ate too many s'mores and then we talked about some crazy cryptology. Chupacabras and Mothmen, indeed! I'm thinking that we're tired and hungry and quite probably dehydrated. We've stumbled into an abandoned salt mine that once used pack animals to carry out the salt, and some local rancher's goats have found their way down here to lick the salt. That's what ruminants do. Ya know, cows and goats and animals that chew their cud. They lick salt!" said Philo.

"That all sounds great! Cousin Philo, you are very good at coming up with reasonable explanations. Except for one small thing. When I entered this chamber, I saw those goats standing up and holding the pick axes. They weren't licking the salt, they were mining it, they were using tools and actually chipping salt from the rocks! I know I've tried to wind you up a lot lately, and it's been fun, the boy who cried wolf and all that, I get it. But I'm sure I saw what I saw. Those goats are miners, and they've also taken Candy!" said an alarmed Shawn in a rapid fire confusion of words.

"I'm not sure what you saw as far as them standing up or using tools, but from what I saw, they didn't just take Candy, they invited her to join them," said Marsha. Looking down at the sandy floor she added, "And she did..."

"Yikes. You guys, we gotta follow them! I don't even care if we find out what the heck is going on down here, I just want to grab Candy and get back to the surface!" said Shawn. "And then make an appointment with a psychiatrist..."

Down the passage way the three teens went in pursuit of Candy and the goats, while up ahead, the goats were gathering together for a conference. They were standing in a circle with the yellow dog in the center, happily trying to engage them in play. Santiago, the small black and brown goat who bade them all leave their tools and walk away, spoke in earnest. "See, I told you there was no way a canine this plump could be a stray, I knew there would be humans coming after her. But no, 'bleaah' you said, 'we've found a protector, bleaah'. Yeah, well bleat to you all, cause now we've got trouble! There have never been humans in this spot. We've got to get away from them. I know we need the protector, and she's such a nice one too, but the humans are more of a threat to us than that... beast... is."

A young brown buck named Basher agreed. "Bleat. But we need their canine. The danger is getting closer all the time. I know I heard the creature when I was on patrol last night. If we don't have a protector, if we can't get a dog, we'll be doomed. It's bad enough that we are always on the run and that we have to travel so far for our lick..."

Salizar agreed. She was the oldest member of the group, the matriarch and keeper of the stories. She had been around long enough to have known goats that lived all their lives above ground. She looked around her at the younger members of the herd and frowned. "We have been living like the hunted for too long now. We Ruminators need the protector. But we need more than that. I am old. You young ones have always been in the caves. You do not know... But I do. I have seen the look in the eyes of those who have played in the sun. Yes, played! This life we lead is no good. Always in the dark, always in fear. We need the protector canine, yes, if we are to keep living like the prairie dogs and worms, but I think we need more." She shifted on her hands and feet and looked down at the ground. "I want to spend days out under the sun lit sky before I die. I am not afraid to approach the humans. Maybe it could be our destruction. But I am willing to take the risk."

Santiago nodded in understanding and agreement. "I do not think they will forget about their canine. Bleat, they will continue after us until we return her to them. That these humans have somehow made their way into our caves may well be a turning point for us. You are right, Salizar, we have lived in fear and hiding for too long. I make a proposal to all gathered here on behalf of the Ruminators. Salizar will return the protector to the humans. If they notice her, baah, differences, then we should give Salizar permission to speak to them and state our case. They may just give us more help than a canine ever could..."

"I am in agreement," said Salizar. "All in favor..."

8 Introductions

Turning a corner, the cousins saw a faint glimpse of the goats far ahead. The tunnel was continuing to go down even further, and it was getting darker once again. The ground beneath their feet was solid rock, no more the sandy floor, and the only sound they heard aside from their breathing was the whir of Philo winding the battery of the flashlight and the smacking sound of their rubber soled hiking boots.

"I'm telling you, something isn't right with these goats," panted Shawn. "I mean, shouldn't we be hearing the clatter of tiny hooves? And what's with them going down deeper? I think we've discovered a rare species of tunneling, tool-using goats!"

"No more jokes, Shawn! This is a rotten time for you to start thinking. We need to get Candy and get out of this mine. I just want to wake up in my little bed back at home!" said Marsha, breathing heavily.

"Hang on," said Philo, "Stop a second. I think I hear something." Philo held out his arm to stop his cousins and had slowed to a walk. He stopped winding his flashlight and cocked his head toward the dark passage. "I'm sure I heard something. Listen."

Quietly, slowly, from out of the darkness ventured an old nanny goat, followed by the golden colored Candy who ran straight to Marsha. The girl happily knelt down to encircle her arms around Candy's neck, overjoyed to see her friend again. While the teens took turns greeting Candy with exclamations of fondness and love, the goat stood patiently off to the side, waiting for them to turn their attention towards her.

The little goat had once been brown in color but was now flecked all over with grey and the hair around her eyes and muzzle had turned such a light grey that it was almost white. Her odd eyes with their rectangular pupils were somewhat clouded by her extreme old age, but she had a pleasant, if somewhat nervous expression as she looked upon the welcome that the humans bestowed on their pet. By all standards she looked like your average elderly nanny goat with what some might notice as an oddly intelligent expression. Until, that is, you looked at her feet…

"Holy houseflies!" shouted Shawn, "Checkout the feet on that goat!"

Salizar nervously shifted her weight from side to side, glancing down at her hands and feet and knowing that they were not what the humans would expect to see at the bottom ends of a goat. The usual bifurcated hoof was replaced in her case by what appeared to be more human than goat, but was not exactly that either. On her front legs, where a modified dew claw would be, there was a tough looking thumb. And instead of the two halves of a cloven hoof, there were four fingers with hoof-like nails. Although roughly calloused, they looked to be perfectly functional hands with large finger nails that were thick and yellow with age, but neatly trimmed. On her back legs the little goat had a similar adaptation. Definitely not hooves, but not quite human feet either. They began higher up the goat's leg, and so were somewhat bigger than human feet. They were elongated, tough and calloused like her hands and with similarly tough nails. Marsha let go of her hold around Candy's neck and began to back away down the passage as her inquisitive cousin Philo approached the creature for a closer look.

"Wowzers, them is some feet you've got, little goat!" Turning back to the others he said, "Gosh, don't be afraid, guys. It may have hands and feet, but it's still just a goat. I'm sure it's unarmed!"

"Philo, that's just the sort of dumb joke I'd expect from Shawn at a time like this. Some of his stupid must be rubbing off on you!" Regaining her confidence and peering at the creature from around her brother, Marsha asked, "Hey, little goat, what the heck happened to you? Shawn, maybe you were right about what you saw back there in the cave..."

Nervously, Salizar looked from one teen to the other as they spoke, weighing her options. Should she just back slowly away and forget the whole idea? Just leave the dog and go? Somehow these human kids didn't react as she had thought they would. From all the stories that she heard, from what her father, old Bezoar, had told her, humans were destructive creatures who at best steal your milk and your young and at worst destroy your mountain home. But these humans hugged and cooed over their canine. They smiled and joked with each other. They were looking at her with interest and not with fear or hatred or hunger.

Salizar swallowed hard and spoke. "Bleeat, um, ah, hello humans. Let me introduce myself. I am known as Salizar. I am the matriarch of the Ruminators, the keeper of their stories, and, bleat, I, ah, need your help."

***

That it took awhile for the kids to get over their surprise at hearing the strange goat with the almost human hands and feet speak is probably an understatement. What made it somewhat easier for them each to wrap their heads around the concept was the sweetly intelligent look on the goat's face and the completely calm demeanor of Candy. Their watch dog, alarm dog, supposed protector was totally at ease with the odd little creature. Eventually, Marsha, Shawn and Philo calmed down enough from their state of shock to start barraging Salizar with questions. Where did you come from? Are you an alien, some sort of mutant? Are the other goats we saw like you? What are you goats doing underground? How is it that you can talk? Can all goats talk?

"No, that's silly," decided Shawn. "Surely we'd have found out by now that goats could talk, right?"

"Silly? You think talking goats are silly? This is all making me feel lightheaded. I can't believe this is actually happening!" declared a decidedly confused Philo.

Meanwhile, Salizar patiently stood there, old and wise enough to know that these human creatures that had been alive longer than any average goat could reasonably expect, were still young for their species and their excitement would eventually subside enough so that she could speak with them. They really did seem to her to be good sorts of humans. Their questions, wild, convoluted and confused, nonetheless showed a great sense of imagination and intelligence and she was reminded of her own grandkids. "Yes," she decided, "I like these young creatures..."

"Are you quite finished, my dears?" she said in a soft low voice. She spoke with a bit of a warble, due to her having evolved from non-speaking bleating goats, and it gave her a grandmotherly sounding voice, reminiscent of homemade cookies and lavender soap, that calmed the three teens down enough so that she might speak. "I can see that you have many questions, which I shall be more than happy to answer. I too have questions, questions for you three, and possibly a favor or two to ask." She paused, looking to the teens for permission. They looked back at Salizar with wide eyes and eager faces, so she continued. "The first question I'd like to ask you is about your names; what are you each called? And my first favor is this: could you possibly not shine that light in my eyes?"

Philo quickly moved the light from the little goat's face and shone it on the ground. "Oh, sorry," he said, totally awed to be talking to a goat. A goat who talked back, no less. "My name's Philo, and these are my cousins. Shawn and Marsha."

"Thank you, Philo, my boy," she said, adding politely, "Delighted, I think, to meet you all. But this dark passageway is no place for civil conversations. What do you say we move our chat to somewhere more comfortable and with better lighting?"

The teens obediently allowed themselves to be led further down the passageway in the same direction that the line of goats had fled earlier. They saw no signs of the rest of the goat herd, who were hiding safely in another chamber. The strange group, humans, dog, and goat, continued through a few twists and turns of the tunnel during which they remained quiet, each deep in his or her own thoughts. The only member of the group that seemed completely at ease with the odd situation was the dog. Candy had accepted the strange goat creatures without prejudice. Although her breeding was a mystery to her human owners, the goats could sense the bit of a herding animal in her, making her protective of her group, combined with enough other miscellaneous breeds of dog to make her friendly, if not particularly bright. The group continued for some minutes before Marsha spoke. "Um, Salizar, is it? Um, any chance we're heading back up to the surface? Ya know, blue skies, fresh air?"

"Sorry, my dear, we for the most part shun the surface world. We have learned that it is not safe for creatures such as us. But we can get you back there, be sure of that. There are many exits to our tunnels. First though, I'd like to have a chat, if you don't mind..."

"Mind?" said Philo, "I'm thrilled. I can't believe what a great vacay I'm having!"

With that, the goat stepped back to let them pass through a doorway into a dimly lit cave. The floor inside was strewn with straw and the dim light was natural, coming through small but very long channels in the ceiling. "Here we are. This is one of our temporary sleeping chambers, for when we are in this area mining. Please, make yourselves comfortable. We have water, but I'm afraid we have nothing that would please a human palate in the way of food. However, I will see what we can do. I would like to answer all of your questions; bleat, I am sure you have many... But before we begin, might you indulge one from me please? Just how exactly did the three of you find your way into our mine?" asked Salizar.

"Aah, well, we weren't intending to, I mean, it wasn't on purpose, if that's what you want to know," said a slightly shaky Shawn. "Our brilliant cousin Philo here, he had us on a camping trip over to Ladron Peak looking for some gold bars that were supposedly hidden here many years ago by some stagecoach robbers."

"Ah, the golden bricks, yes, we know of them. They are pretty. Shiny and bright, but they serve no purpose. They are not even good enough for use in building anything! Far too heavy and somewhat soft," explained Salizar shaking her head.

"You've seen them? They are real?" exclaimed a satisfied Philo. "See, my good cousins, I did not lead you on such a wild goose chase after all!"

"More like a wild goat chase if you ask me!" Shawn glanced at their host and frowned when he saw the look on Salizar's face. "Oh sorry, I didn't mean anything by it. Marsha and Philo will tell you I'm pretty good at making inappropriate jokes. Plus, it's been a bit of a weird day." Shawn paused, reflecting on what he just said. Calling it a weird day was definitely an understatement. "So you really have seen the gold bars? That's great! Maybe you can tell us where they are and we'll take 'em off your, ahem, hands... and be on our way... Gee, I'm getting hungry."

"Don't mind my brother, Salizar, like he says, he's often a bit rudely inappropriate... and always a bit hungry too!" Marsha picked up a piece of straw and absentmindedly put it in her mouth to chew on. "...So yeah, we were out walking around and looking for the gold, and there was a big rumble and the ground just opened up beneath our feet and we all fell in." At hearing this, the goat looked concerned and shook her head slightly. "Philo thinks it was a cave in of your mine caused by that earthquake and some minerals that were weakening the rock. Didn't you feel it? Anyway, for some reason, we couldn't get back out again. So we followed your light. But look, we're not intending to stay, if that's what's worrying you, although I for one am really interested in hearing more about you... I can't believe I'm saying this, but finding the gold and getting back to the surface can wait as far as I'm concerned. Shawn, you know you couldn't buy this experience for all the gold in, well, Ladron Peak!"

Book Two - Salizar

1 The Hot Wind

Salizar looked at the earnest expressions on the faces of her guests. "Do not worry, young humans," she said. "You will be safely back home soon. And with the golden bricks if you like. Baah, they are around here somewhere... I only ask that perhaps you could listen to a bit of our history and consider our plight. The Ruminators have lived underground and in fear for almost as long as we have been in existence, and we would like to ask for your help..."

"Who are the Ruminators and how can we help them?" asked Marsha with a note of concern in her voice.

Well," began Salizar with a slightly weird warble to her voice, the answers to those questions are contained in our story. It's rather long story. To explain may take awhile... with your permission... but first, we may as well get comfy. Bleaat." The old goat gestured for the teens to sit or lie down in the straw, and then she herself sat down. She crouched down on her haunches, like you would expect any ordinary goat to sit, even though she was far from ordinary. Her bare back feet, looking somewhat like the elongated feet of an elderly woman who had never known shoes, were flat to the ground at her sides, with her hands resting, knuckles entwined, in front of her. She then settled down with some difficulty, perhaps due to arthritis, onto her stomach, and Marsha couldn't help but wonder what it must be like to be an intelligent creature in such a strange and ungainly body. Just the thought of having udders like that made her feel quite uncomfortable.

"It always looks so soft in the movies," said Shawn, trying to get over just how very poky the straw was. After attempting to wad the stuff up into a comfortable lump to lean on, he gave up and leant instead against the hard rock wall. Salizar offered the teens a bowl of water and they passed it around, finally placing it in on the ground in front of Candy, who emptied it quickly with her sloppy lapping. Then the dog went off into the corner near Salizar and turned around in a circle several times to create a nest in the straw. Putting her head down on her paws, she drifted instantly off to sleep. Shawn took notice of Candy's nest making technique and tried it for himself, kicking up a cloud of straw in the enclosed space, and earning a frown from his sister. Shawn couldn't understand why she was always so bossy. "Jeez, Marsha," he said in reply, "sometimes you are worse than Mom. You'll make someone a very controlling mother one day..."

Salizar waited while they all got situated. She couldn't help but be nervous, having three humans so near by. When Shawn's dust had finally settled, she spoke. "If there are no objections, I will begin our story. I know you have questions about who the Ruminators are and how we came to be, and I think the easiest way to answer them is to start at the beginning, at our creation."

"Creation?" asked Shawn, "isn't that a bit too far back? Can't you just start with when you guys learned to talk and grew human parts?"

Marsha jabbed him in the ribs with her elbow. She couldn't help but try to guide her little brother. She'd always done it, treating him in a motherly way since they were small. "Sorry, Salizar, my brother has been spending this summer vacation practicing for the dope of the year tryouts…"

Salizar looked quizzically at the two of them, not quite understanding what it was that the girl was trying to say. She decided that Marsha was probably apologizing once again for her brother's flippant remarks, and she continued. "No

85

problem, my dear Marsha. Bleaat. But Shawn, our history, well, that is, the creation of the Ruminators, did not occur so very long ago. We are a rather new species of creature, created before my time, and certainly before your time, but a species recently born." Salizar was nervous. She was having a hard time coming up with the correct words, wanting very much to be understood by these human creatures and she was trying not to interject bleating sounds into her conversation. "We were created in a relatively recent moment of history. A moment of your human history. You see, it was you that made us."

"It all started in about the middle of the last century. Your people, and by that I mean human beings, were at war with one another. Since the time of our Awakening we have sadly come to understand that this is a rather normal state of affairs... Anyway, in the course of events, the humans were trying to come up with ways to better kill one another. My people, and by that I mean goats, were the servants of man, supplying milk and meat in exchange for food and protection. My direct descendants belonged to a herd that lived in the hills south of here, around the land of white."

Shawn interrupted to clarify for Philo. "I think she means White Sands. It's both a National Monument and an active Missile Range. A place for picnics and war games, I guess." Turning back to Salizar, Shawn pointed at Philo and said, "He's not from around here."

"Oh, thank you, Shawn, bleat. Please, feel free to interrupt at any time if what I say is unclear..." Salizar unfolded her hands and reached out to pet the sleeping Candy, who appeared to be dreaming, chasing an imaginary jack rabbit. Folding her hands back in front of her, the old goat took a deep breath and began to speak again. "Early one morning, before the sun had risen, the herd was just waking up and thinking about their breakfast when the sky lit up as bright as midday but with all colors of the rainbow. Goats do not normally perceive much in the way of color, but that day the legend says that they saw them all. The ground shook and a rush of hot wind blew over and frightened the herd. Baah. Goats of the ancient kind were not much prone to pondering things, other than the basic necessities such as which kind of bush tastes better or where to find the best shade tree at what time of day and so just as suddenly as this hot wind occurred, it was over and all but forgotten. The goats got on with the business of their day and for the most part the herd thought no more about it."

"Bleat, but something in the hot wind changed the herd. In the days and weeks that followed the strange predawn wind, some of the herd got sick and died. Not all, but some. And other goats, well, one day early in the winter, a young female goat who had been carrying finally delivered her kid. The mother goat was sorely late and had been expected to deliver almost three months sooner, but no kid came. She wasn't the only goat in the herd that was having an extremely long gestation, and something odd had been happening to each of the prospective mothers as their pregnancies went on longer and longer. For lack of a better way to put it, I'll just tell you, bleat, that the goats got smarter. Not the whole herd mind you. Like I said, some of the herd died after a terrible illness and some just stayed as they were. But those that were carrying a kid, the pregnant goats, they became more and more aware of their surroundings. Bleat. They began to notice the things in the world around them that weren't just there to provide the daily necessities of sustenance and shelter. They began to notice things that were purely pleasurable, like the colors of a beautiful sunset, the smell of the air after it rains, or the sound made by a breeze moving through the leaves of a tree." Salizar smiled and closed her eyes momentarily, as though she was feeling that breeze in her face.

"The pregnant goats also found that they began to be receptive to human speech, that they could actually understand what the rancher and his family were talking about. They soon discovered that they had to leave the ranch. Our ancestors overheard some human visitors say that the entire herd was going to be destroyed because of something called 'exposure'. The visitors said that their milk was bad and that their meat would be too. And so, one by one, or in groups of two, so as not to be noticed, the pregnant goats began disappearing. They headed south, baah, to a small cave that they found where they could give birth to their kids and consider their situation. The refugees and their babies formed a new herd, which they later named the Ruminators because they found their new abilities of cognition, their ability to contemplate their very existence, to be a most wonderful gift. Bleat."

"Hang on, at the risk of saying something dumb, doesn't ruminate mean to chew?" asked Shawn.

"Yes, to chew, both physically and mentally. To chew the cud and to mull over a thought. To ponder..." said Salizar. "Like our ancestors were doing in their little cave. Wondering what to do next. A group of pregnant goats, on their own, without a human to keep and feed them. It was a wonderful and confusing time for them. Freedom by definition is liberating, but it can also be frightening. Having no choice is a terrible thing, but suddenly having options when you have never had any before, well... scary." Philo nodded in agreement, as though it was a topic that he had given some thought to, or perhaps had researched.

Salizar continued. "It was early winter when the first kid was born. The little cave provided enough protection from the weather, and the temperatures were not extreme. There was adequate vegetation available for the small group and though water was not plentiful, it was sufficient. When the females that were in the early stages of pregnancy during that dawn of the hot wind, when they finally delivered, it was plain to see that their babies had some notable and surprising differences. The newborn kids were far from ordinary. Baah, the most initially obvious difference between the babies and their mothers was, of course, their hands and feet. You have seen what mine look like... bleat. The first kids born after the event had a similar mutation of the extremities, which has only continued to improve in function in subsequent generations. In addition, we have each gained a longer life. A normal goat's life span is about ten to twelve years, but we now find ourselves living much longer. I am nearing forty, and you can see I am getting quite old. So it has only been three or four generations of the Ruminators that bring us to today; to our present refinement of hands and feet. I am only second generation and my hands and feet are quite useful as you can see. Though we do miss out on the traditional goats' abilities to clamber on rock without the cuts or calluses..."

Shawn couldn't resist commenting on Salizar's observation by holding up his own foot to show off his hiking boot. "What you guys need are a few pairs of these! Make life much easier!" He fully expected Marsha to give him a jab, or at least a withering look after he said it and he let out a small nervous laugh, still holding his foot up in the air, when no such comment came.

Salizar politely acknowledged the advice, like she would if he were one of the kids in her herd. "Thank you, Shawn, we shall work on that idea." She then took the opportunity to pause and shift her weight, repositioning herself in the straw. The three human teens, Shawn included, were enthralled during the telling of the goats' history. While Salizar spoke, the occasional bleat and waver in her voice betrayed the fact that it was a goat doing the talking, but the underground chamber was so quiet otherwise that only the breathing of the sleeping Candy could be heard. "Perhaps," Salizar said, "we should take a break here.

If you like, you may ask questions about what I have said. I have never had occasion to speak to humans; perhaps my telling of the story is not so clear."

"You are remarkably well spoken, Salizar," said Marsha, emphasizing the word 'remarkably.' "Please continue. I would love to hear more. I'm particularly interested to find out how your, um, people, acquired speech. Can't you please continue with your story? I'd really like to know how it happened."

"Marsha, I am deeply flattered by your interest. Flattered and heartened that you may hear our tale and decide to help us. But this is a long story. I believe I need to get up and stretch my withers." Salizar swiveled her head on her long goat neck, stood up and began to walk around the chamber. "If you don't mind, I'm going to speak to the rest of my herd; just to reassure them that all is well. They must be worried. I shan't be long. Make yourselves comfortable, stretch, have some water. I'll be right back." With that, she slowly walked off into the dark passageway.

2 On The Radio

It was a beautiful day for a drive, as long as the air conditioner was working, and Trudy smiled, enjoying the blue sky scenery and thinking about the fun she was going to have surprising the kids. She could see hazy blue mountains off in the distance and the green swath of the Rio Grande river valley to the east. In the west, more blue and purple mountains and yellow sandstone mesas. Trudy thought about how Marsha always liked to start each morning with the comment, "another beautiful day in paradise" and although she said it almost every day, it was almost always true. Trudy sighed. If only Frank were still around to share it with them. He was always ready to pack up the truck and head out to a National Forest or State Park. Frank would camp out any time of the year, in any weather. "Just like the post office," Trudy thought, "neither rain nor sleet nor gloom of night, or however that saying went..." She remembered back to a time when they were courting. He had somehow managed to convince her to go camping in January.

She'd never forget having to chip the ice off of the outside of the cooler that they'd had to use to keep their fruit and veggies from freezing.

Tuning the radio to KUNM, Trudy just caught the end of the midday news report. "…small livestock and pets being drained of their blood and left for dead. Residents wonder if it could it be satanic rituals, aliens or the fabled chu-…" The report turned to static as the pickup truck went through a pass carved out of the rock mesa and the signal was lost. Trudy didn't bother to retune the station, knowing that she would drive out of the pass again in a few seconds. When eventually the static cleared, the same announcer's voice was heard. "… in possibly related news, earlier today, an agent with the Socorro County Animal Control was found dead of unknown causes. The man, who has not been named, was in the field investigating a bear sighting, but no apparent evidence of a bear was found. Results from an autopsy will be forthcoming. That concludes the midday news, and coming up next on KUNM, your New Mexico public radio, Freeform Jazz!"

***

When Salizar had been gone out of the cave for a few moments, Marsha broke the silence. "Okay, somebody pinch me, I must be dreaming. Ow, Shawn! You know I didn't mean it literally!" Marsha was forced to rub her shoulder where the offending pinch had occurred. "This is absolutely, positively, the weirdest thing that has ever happened in the whole history of this planet!" She gave Shawn a sisterly punch in the arm, but not before he flinched in anticipation of the blow. "The bigger you get, Shawn, the harder a target you are to hit!"

"See, I've learned something after living with you all these years! I always know when you're about to hit me... maybe I can read your mind!" Shawn wiggled his fingers in Marsha's face as he said this and made an eerie noise. "I'll bet I can even hypnotize you into thinking that you are in an underground cave listening to stories told by a weird old goat." Shawn stretched out his pronunciation of the word goat so that it sounded spooky, then sat bolt upright with a blank stare on his face and said, "Hey, wait a minute, maybe it's you who have hypnotized me!"

"Ooh, I am under your spell. I hear talking goats too," said Philo in a robotic voice. Returning to his normally enthusiastic tone Philo added, "But I must admit, I think I'm enjoying this hallucination! I can't wait until Salizar gets back and continues her story. How in the world did they learn to speak? And what do the Ruminators need help with? What kind of help could we possibly provide?"

Candy woke up from her nap, lifted her head from her paws and sniffed the air. The dog then stood up and walked over to the chamber's entrance, looking out into the dark tunnel. A moment later, Salizar walked into the cave. She bowed slightly to the three teens, bending one knee (or was it an elbow?), as a way of greeting them. "The herd was happy to hear that you are

94

not a threat to our existence. They are actually quite anxious to meet you, to meet some actual human beings. But first, I'd like to continue with our story if I might. Please, again, feel free to ask questions if you like."

Salizar lowered and shifted her body, trying to get comfortable in the straw again. It was obvious that at nearly forty years of age, she was extremely old for a goat and no matter what kind of mutations these creatures had gone through, it was affecting her body. "Before I went to check on the others, we were talking about language, the acquisition of language. Now, the new generation, those born after the hot wind washed over the herd, not only did they have their mothers' abilities of comprehension and wonder, but they also had the rudimentary physical qualities necessary for speech. But you may well wonder how it was that the next generation learned to speak when their mothers were, by all physical means, incapable of forming language," Salizar said, holding up an index finger and waving it back and forth to accent her point. "Being physically capable of speech does not equal speaking if there is no one to teach you how!"

"Of course, the mothers could make the usual bleating sounds, which do serve goats well when talking about those things universal to ancient goats. For example there are different bleats that mean 'Danger!' or 'Food!' or 'Where's my kid?' or convey messages of that nature. But when these new kinds of goat found that they wanted to say 'look at that beautiful flower' or 'my, doesn't this sun feel delicious' they were at a complete loss. No goats had ever wanted to say those things before. However, these goats most certainly did, and they wanted their offspring to say these things too. It was definitely an odd time for these creatures. We refer to that time now as the Awakening."

"So how did they teach their kids to speak? What even made them think they could?" asked Philo. "I mean, before the goats had left their herd they had listened to humans talking, but their kids hadn't heard anyone speak growing up in a cave. So how did it happen?"

"You ask some excellent questions, my boy. Again, it was the forward progress of your kind that provided us with the means to learn to speak. Language came to the Ruminators with an invention, a gadget, a human advance if you will. The Ruminators learned to speak because humans developed the transistor radio."

Shawn looked puzzled. "Humans developed the what?"

Salizar repeated herself. "The transistor radio. Maybe you don't know it, Shawn? It is a gadget, a little box that can portably receive radio signals."

Philo interrupted. "Oh, Shawn, it was long before our time! I believe the transistor was developed about the same time as Salizar's ancestors experienced the blast, the hot wind, that, you know, changed them." Philo frowned, not liking the sound of what he just said, but he continued. "A transistor is a kind of

96

little electronic switch that is contained in lots of devices. Not just radios. Calculators and computers have them too. Transistors amplify electronic signals, making them more powerful. It was essential in making radios smaller and therefore portable. Before transistors were developed, they used vacuum tubes which were these big clunky glass things. Definitely not for lugging around on picnics or trips to the beach. Or could you imagine? Jogging, wearing a radio with vacuum tubes? Ha! Nowadays, transistors are really tiny things that are part of integrated circuits, you know, computer chips."

"Well, young Philo, you certainly are a knowledgeable human," complimented Salizar.

"Yeah, he's a regular walking transistor!" laughed an amused Shawn, reaching over to pat his cousin on the head. Philo smiled back, pleased that he might yet atone for his iron pyrite mistake.

"Yes, well, it was about ten years after the Awakening that a radio was found…bleat… But wait, I need to go back a bit. That first kid that was born after the blast was a male named Bezoar. He was the smartest and most inquisitive goat that had ever walked the earth. His mother died when he was young, she had a regular goat's life span, about twelve years old she was. He was perhaps only two or three years old, but he stayed with the Ruminators and eventually grew to be a sort of leader of the group… as well as becoming my father." Salizar stopped to

97

smile, looking as though she were experiencing a pleasant memory of her childhood.

"When Bezoar was in his teen years, he enjoyed exploring the desert hills and mountain forests, sometimes being gone for days at a time. It was on one of these trips that he came upon a hunting cabin in a wooded area. The cabin belonged to a man and his son who would come up on weekends during hunting season from a place called Carslbad to hunt elk. My father liked to visit the cabin regularly, always at sundown when the humans were having their meal and always keeping well hidden. He enjoyed listening to the conversation between the father and son and managed to acquire some language from them. The Ruminators were quite surprised the first time Bezoar returned from listening to the hunters and bleated out a few rough words of English. It was unfortunate that his own mother was no longer alive to hear him speak, but there was still two or three of the original group of mothers around, and they were very proud."

"Do you happen to know what were the first words spoken by your father?' asked Shawn.

"Yes, apparently he returned from one such trip observing the men and said the phrase 'church key'. Later he told me that these words held some special meaning for the humans, but we have yet to discover what it is. We think it may have some sort of spiritual significance. A church is the place where humans worship their god, is it not? And a key opens doors…?"

Philo chuckled. "I feel sorry to tell you this, but a 'church key' is kind of a disused term for a bottle opener. Once upon a time, canned drinks didn't have pull tabs, and bottled ones didn't twist off. A special opener was needed. I imagine that your father witnessed these guys coming back to their cabin after a hard day's hunting, wanting to have a few beers and losing their opener." Salizar frowned, and Philo felt she needed a bit more information on the ways of humans. "Beer is an alcoholic beverage that some adult humans enjoy. It makes them drunk, ya know, and they can act kind of silly or stupid."

A light went on in Salizar's eyes and she smiled. "Ah yes, there is a plant in these foothills. Chewing the leaves causes a similar effect among our people. Silly or stupid, yes. That certainly does explain a few things... A church key..." Salizar paused and looked thoughtful before continuing. "These men actually managed to burn down their own cabin one night. Bezoar saw it happen. He was there, eavesdropping at the window, and the men were inside, looking for the church key, rummaging around, when one of the men knocks over a lantern. Father said that the lantern ignited a pile of blankets. Apparently the men, silly or stupid perhaps, took off running, and did not try to stop the fire. Instead, they grabbed their guns and a few other items, climbed in their vehicle and drove off. In their haste to escape, they dropped a small transistor radio which Bezoar picked up and took back to the Ruminators. Luckily the fire didn't burn down the forest. It only destroyed the cabin. And one of my father's favorite eavesdropping spots. But now he had a new hobby... learning to speak... because it was that little transistor radio which brought true speech to our kind."

"I figured that you couldn't have learned all of your vocabulary from having your dad eavesdrop on two guys in a cabin. I mean, you are very well spoken!" complimented Marsha again. Salizar looked pleased and nodded her head in appreciation, as Marsha posed another question, looking for clarification. "So Bezoar took the radio back and the Ruminators listened to it and then learned to speak?"

"It's kind of a funny story, really. When Bezoar first brought the 'magic box' back to the cave where the herd sheltered at night, the Ruminators were afraid of it. They couldn't get over the sounds that came out. The Ruminators would gather each evening after they had done their chores and they would listen and learn. But what they first learned was music! Country and western music! Hank Snow, George Jones, Hank Williams... You see, Bezoar had seen the hunters moving the knobs around, but he didn't want to try it himself for fear of losing the sounds. So the first sentence that many of the goats spoke was 'you ain't nothing but a hound dog'. After a time, of course, the batteries of that little radio gave out, but not before my father picked up the nerve to turn the little knob and change the station."

"The first time the Ruminators got to hear a news broadcast, it was a revelation for them. They found out things about the humans living across New Mexico and America, and about things happening in the greater world that they never could have found out about otherwise. The Ruminators became aware of just how much they did not know, and so Bezoar and a few of the other young males began to plan information gathering missions. They would go to nearby villages, always staying hidden, to eavesdrop on the residents and try to find out what was happening, and also to learn more words. They would often go at night, and hide under windows, listening... It was during one of these missions that Bezoar's best friend, a goat named Gizmo, overheard two ranchers talking about some problem that they were having with their goat herds. ...And our world changed. Again." Salizar frowned and sat up to pour herself a bowl full of water, holding it in her two hands, but lapping at it like any ordinary goat.

3 Eavesdropper

The little goat Gizmo went to visit his friend Bezoar. Although the two goats were both part of that first new generation with their human looking hands and feet, they couldn't be more different in appearance from each other. They were nearly the same age, with Gizmo having been born just a few months after his friend, but Gizmo had a delicate appearance that caused many of the nanny goats to continuously fuss over him as though he were a baby. Gizmo was small, with apricot-colored fur so wiry it was almost curly and pretty wide brown eyes with long lashes. Bezoar in contrast, was an exceptionally sturdy buck, with a physique built of solid muscle. He stood several inches taller than Gizmo and was almost totally black in color except for a white blaze down his nose. The two were the best of friends, but while Bezoar liked adventure as much as Gizmo, he was less of a risk taker. In spite of his physique, Bezoar was prone to using what was in his skull rather than the horns sprouting from it, preferring planning and stealth to boldness and brawn. It might have been because Gizmo endured so much coddling by the older females that he became so adventurous, desiring to prove he was a tough and capable buck, and not just a cute little kid. On the night in question, Gizmo, as always, was in the mood for a bit of exploring and eavesdropping and was intent on getting his friend to join him. "C'mon, Bezoar, it's an awfully nice night. I thought we could go over to that ranch just near the foothills. Those old guys tell some pretty funny jokes! Whaddya say?"

Bezoar shook his dark head. "Can't, Giz. I gotta stay with the herd. Cousin Dolores is probably going to have her kid tonight, and the women want me to stay close by so that they can focus on Dolores without having to worry about predators. I'm thinking maybe you should stick around and help out too... Let the ladies fuss over you instead of Dolores so that she can have her kid in peace! Besides, it would be good if you didn't get into any trouble while I'm otherwise occupied."

"Bezoar! You can be such a jerk! I don't need you to get me out of trouble! I can get myself out of trouble! Um, I mean, bleat, I won't get into any trouble!" Gizmo glared angrily at his friend and lowered his head as an indication that he might like to strike him with his horns. Then Gizmo uttered a phrase that he had learned from listening to the old ranchers. "You're not the boss of me!" he shouted.

"Aww, Giz, I'm sorry, I only meant... Can't you wait 'til tomorrow night, when I can come with you?"

Gizmo didn't reply, but instead let out an angry sounding bleat and stormed away, determined to carry out his plans for the evening with or without Bezoar.

***

The two elderly ranchers were neighbors and had been for a long time. They enjoyed spending time in the evenings with each other, taking turns sitting on each other's porches and sharing stories about their youth, laughing and telling jokes and talking about their day. This particular night was no different, with their wives sitting together in the kitchen over cups of tea and the two men sitting on the porch, one leaning back in a chair and the other perched down on the steps. The men were discussing some odd things that had been happening to their smaller livestock, goats in particular. When they got to talking about it, the men discovered that they both had been missing some members of their herds and, what was worse, each had found a few carcasses.

This certainly was terrible news, and not at all like the jokes and tall tales that Gizmo had wanted to hear. He was hiding around the corner of the house, behind a cottonwood tree so as to keep out of the porch light's glow. As quietly and stealthily as he could, Gizmo crept closer to better hear what they were saying. At just that moment, the wife of the house had set a plate of homemade butter cookies in front of her friend and turned to switch off the light that illuminated the kitchen sink. She happened to glance out the open window and something caught her eye in the darkened yard. There, light colored fur glowing in the moonlight, crept the little goat Gizmo. "Goat on the go!" she shouted, and Gizmo ran for his life with the men running after him. Luckily for Gizmo, the ranchers were rather old and not terribly committed to the chase that was interrupting their evening relaxation, so the little goat got away with his heart pounding.

When Gizmo got back and told the rest of the Ruminators what he had heard, Bezoar naturally thought that it was very important that they find out what was happening to the ranchers' livestock. He decided that they should go back again the next night, he and Gizmo together, and see if they could learn anything more.

***

Timidly into the chamber walked a small young goat with a white coat that grew in short whorls. The newcomer looked shyly at the humans and back to Salizar who assured her with a small bleat that all was well. Turning to the humans, Salizar introduced the little goat as Nougat. "Nougat is my daughter's daughter. Part of the newest generation of the Ruminators. She is in terms of maturity what I believe you call a teenager?"

Nougat rolled her odd goat eyes. "Oh, Gramma..." she said. Then turning nervously to the humans she smiled. It was odd to see a goat smile and it made the three teens giggle. The sound of laughter reassured and emboldened the little goat and she bowed, bending one knee, and spoke. "I am very pleased to meet you all. I have only seen your kind once before, and that was from a great distance. I am so very happy to get to talk with you. Close up."

"Trust me, we are pretty doggone excited to get the chance to be close up to you too, Nougat!" said Philo, who proceeded to introduce himself and his cousins. "It seems that you are at somewhat of an advantage. You had seen us from a distance, but we did not even know that your kind existed!"

"Yeah, and your grandmother was telling us some stories about how the Ruminators came to be. All about your great-granddad and his BFF the Giz, and we are finding the stories incredibly fantastic. But Salizar, do you think you could finish up? We really do need to get back up top," said Shawn, adding, "I'm getting hungry."

"My dear Shawn, I have arranged to have some food brought in that I hope will be acceptable to you. We do go on the occasional, bleat, ahem, exploratory jaunts, and the young members of the herd especially enjoy bringing back human oddities. It's quite probable that the food that I am having brought in for you are your very own provisions. Please know that we are not thieves. Although it is true, we sometimes do take things that we do not really need, unless you consider the great need we have to explore, discover and learn about the world."

Nougat took a small step forward. "I have ventured to taste a bit of what we assume to be human foods. Some of the things I have tried have turned out not to be edible, so maybe we are interpreting the pictures on the packages incorrectly," said Nougat.

Marsha laughed. "No, Nougat, you should see some of the things that pass for food as far as Shawn is concerned. He is the absolute king of the chemical laboratory! If a snack food lists an ingredient that is not found in a home kitchen, Shawn is sure to like it. Even more so if it is unpronounceable!" Marsha joked, adding, "The more unnatural the color the better!

"Hey, Sis, how come you're always picking on me? I always thought it was goats that'll eat anything. They always show them in cartoons eating tin cans!" said Shawn.

Salizar looked shocked. "Goats eating tin cans!? That's ridiculous!"

Nougat giggled, finding her grandmothers' overreaction to be rather humorous. "I would love to read the labels on the cans, but not eat the cans themselves! I am sorry that I am unable to read the words on the things we find. Perhaps if you are staying with us, you could give me lessons?" posed Nougat.

"I don't know about teaching you to read," said Shawn, "but we could probably find a can opener for you!"

Salizar gave Nougat a look that said 'enough', but resisted giving the same look to Shawn. Then she cleared her throat, bleated once and began to speak. "So. Getting back to our story. Just where was I?"

"Um, Bezoar and Gizmo were just going to pay another visit to the rancher's house. To find out what was happening to the ranchers' livestock," reminded Philo.

"That's right. Well, the two brave young goats went out together the next night to see if the old ranchers were sitting and talking and enjoying their evening as usual. Bezoar, as you remember, had a cooler and more cautious head than Gizmo and was less prone to taking risks, so he was quite alarmed when they got near to the rancher's house and some sort of gathering was going on. Several pickup trucks were parked haphazardly all over the dirt yard and the sight of so many vehicles meant that there would be way too many people around for Bezoar to approach. But Bezoar sensed from what Gizmo had told him that there was something out of the ordinary going on and that they should take the risk. They determined that as long as they stuck to the dark side of the house and didn't make a sound they should be able to listen to whatever the humans were talking about. The excess of trucks could even provide them with some cover should they need to run or hide.

There were about eight or nine men in the front room and about as many women back in the kitchen. With the porch light blazing, the two bucks knew that they would be better concealed listening in at the kitchen window around back, even though Gizmo knew he had already been sighted once through that window."

"Okay, so what did they hear?" asked an impatient Shawn.

"The women were asking the rancher's wife about what was going on in the front room with the men. Apparently get-togethers were unusual for these humans except when they needed each other to fight fires or mend fences or at branding time, so this was out of the ordinary and the women were worried. The rancher's wife tells them that something has been killing their livestock, especially the smaller animals, the sheep and goats, and a couple of the women nod that yes, it's been happening to their animals as well. One of the women says that her husband thinks there must be wolves in the area, which of course causes Bezoar and Gizmo to become quite alarmed."

"At this point in time, the Ruminators were still living above ground and sheltering at night in some small caves. They had Bezoar and a few other big males as some sort of security, but even the biggest goat is no match for a wolf! But then the wife tells the women that her husband has seen the creature and according to him 'it weren't no wolf'. At hearing this, Bezoar and Gizmo, who are hiding in the shadows just under the kitchen window, look at each other quizzically and Gizmo whispers 'what could it be?' And just as he says this, the woman names the beast. She calls it 'The Chupacabra', almost whispers the name, with fright and reverence in her voice. Gizmo gasps

109

audibly, even though he has never heard the word, but the way the woman says the word 'chupacabra' fills him with fear."

"Luckily, Gizmo's gasp is drowned out by the sound of all the women in the kitchen sitting back and laughing and saying things like 'don't be silly' and 'no such thing'. But the rancher's wife assures them that her husband has seen it with his own eyes! Sucking the life out of one of their goats! Of course Bezoar and Gizmo were frightened and confused. They were the supposed target of this creature, this chupacabra, this goat-killer, but what was it, where was it, what did it look like? The humans in the kitchen seemed quite familiar with the chupacabra, but most of them were apparently skeptical about whether or not such a creature even existed."

4 On The Mountain

Trudy steered her truck into her neighbors' driveway, happy that they had left the gate open. She had always hated gates, having to get out of the truck to open one, get back in and drive through, get out again and close it. It reminded her of the joke about three guys riding in a pickup truck, the question being, which guy is the real cowboy? The answer, of course, is the guy in the middle. He doesn't have to drive, and he doesn't have to get out and open any gates. Some people who lived out here on the edge of nowhere were getting solar powered gates that operated with something like a garage door opener. Just press a button, gate swings open. Great. Before Trudy had time to remember, she thought, "I'll have to get Frank to install one for me..."

Loretta came out of the house at the sound of Trudy's truck in her yard. She waved hello and waited on the porch while Trudy walked toward her. "No, I haven't heard from the kids, not a peep. Here let me get the walkie-talkie for you." She went into the house and came back out before the door had time to swing all the way shut. "Hey Trudy! Did you feel that earthquake while you were down in Socorro? The earth really rumbled. Happened right after you left..."

"No, I didn't! I must have been in the car. But SaraJane didn't mention anything, and I didn't hear anything on the radio either. Are you sure it was an earthquake? You know, I sometimes wonder about all the strange booms we feel around here. It could be some sort of weapons testing on the Army's part; you know they're always training or testing or refueling something here." Trudy gestured towards the sky above their heads and the New Mexico landscape in general. "I wish the military wouldn't look at the desert southwest as just someplace desolate to test weapons or dump waste. It's a beautiful thriving environment." Trudy let out a sigh. "Sorry to go off on my tangent, Loretta... Anyway, thanks for keeping an ear out, I think I'm going to try and go over there and join them. Enjoy some of that beautiful thriving desert environment! Would you mind feeding my chickens again tomorrow? And of course take any eggs. We should be back day after."

Loretta agreed, declaring it 'no problem' and Trudy turned to go, shouting "Thanks again, Loretta!" over her shoulder. She climbed into the cab of the truck and started the engine. After politely closing Loretta and Carlos' front gate, Trudy tried to call the kids on the walkie-talkie, but to no avail. "That's odd," she thought, "these dumb things are supposed to work over a really long range. Oh, I'll bet they've turned it off or left it behind. Marsha and Shawn are getting all independent on me. Had to happen sooner or later. Why not later?" Trudy shook her head to banish thoughts of loneliness and missing Frank. Again. He really hadn't been gone long enough for the shock to have worn off. Trudy still had the nagging feeling that she had missed some clue as to why and where he had gone. He hadn't been unhappy at work or at home, and the family had plans for a skiing trip over the Thanksgiving break. Frank was really looking forward to that. If only he would get in contact! The not knowing was rough, especially on the kids. "Well," she thought, deciding against going home first, "I've already packed my toothbrush. I'll just drive over and find them. It shouldn't be hard. Not much to hide behind up there. I should be able to find those bright yellow tents even without the walkie-talkie."

***

"Oh jeez," said Shawn with disdain in his voice, "chupacabras! They are just mythical creatures. Something that we New Mexicans use to scare our big city, out-of-town, visiting cousins with. I hope you guys didn't believe those crazy ranchers!"

"Yes, Shawn, we do believe them," said Salizar in a reverential voice. "It's not just what the ranchers said they saw, not just a matter of us taking their word for it, but I have seen them too! Chupacabras do exist, and they are as horrible as the stories say they are!" Salizar shuddered at the thought.

"Oh, come on," said Marsha, "Shawn and I have lived here all our lives and we've never heard any serious reports. I was just telling Philo that whenever people say they have found one it's always some mangy dead dog or coyote!"

"Well, this story I'm telling you happened down south. South of the town of Alamogordo. It's one reason why the Ruminators have come as far north as they have. But now we have reason to believe that the chupacabras have followed us. Or, at least, that they are making migrations in the same direction," said a solemn Salizar.

"Okay, wait a minute," said Philo, looking for a reason to believe Salizar's story. "When you say chupacabra, what exactly are you talking about? You say you've seen one? Can you actually describe it for us?"

Salizar gave another shudder and turned to her granddaughter. "Nougat," she said, "would you please go and see what is keeping your brother? He is supposed to be bringing some food for our guests." As soon as she was sure that Nougat had gone, Salizar let out a sigh and said "Okay, the chupacabra. Well, I'll try to describe what I saw. It's truly horrible to think about, but, bleat, I'll try." Candy seemed to sense her new friend's disquiet and she moved closer to the elderly goat and leaned her body against Salizar reassuringly. "When I first saw the creature, it was some years ago. I was out browsing for food, and I had just come around from behind a clump of pinon trees where I had been concentrating on the wonderful nuts that had fallen to the

114

ground. Pinon nutshells are so hard, but their meats are so delicious. So I was distracted, working to free the tiny morsels. The nuts had fallen into the rather dense underbrush, so I wasn't aware of the creature's presence. I shall never forget the sight of it, when I looked up and saw it curled around a jackrabbit. It was shaking the hare by its neck, poor thing, and I let out a bleat of shock and surprise. I couldn't help it! I felt so devastated, helpless, so upset for the jackrabbit. Losing its life like that. But it could have been me... It could have been me." Salizar hung her head and paused a moment, thinking about the poor jackrabbit and her own narrow escape.

"The creature that I saw was not unlike what the woman in the kitchen described her husband as seeing. Bleat, it was not large, not large like a wolf, but rather it was about the size of a coyote or of Candy here, but shaped differently, with more massive shoulders and front legs. It had strange fur, like no fur at all, really, or like really greasy fur, I'm not exactly sure which. I saw it just for a few seconds. The chupacabra's back was big and hunched over and I could see its spine very clearly. The bones along its back were very pointy, or maybe it had spines sticking out of its back, all the way down its back, ending in a thin whip of a tail. But what was really frightening was the face! The creature had a long pointy snout with sharp teeth. Like a pack rat's face, but with a much pointier nose and with sharp teeth that seemed too numerous to count. But the worst part, bleat, those enormous hungry eyes! It turned and looked at me, still with the hare in its mouth and I saw its eyes! Bleaah, horrible,

horrible, I tell you! I had a hard time not fainting! Those eyes! Huge, they were, black and shining, good for seeing in the dark I imagine, and far apart on the skull. It looked right at me and I backed away, and then... I ran for my life."

All through the description of the chupacabra, Candy cuddled in close to her new friend and closed her eyes. Salizar bleated softly to her and stroked her ears. "I know it's hard for you to believe, but it is the truth. And what is worse, that first time I saw the chupacabra was not the last. After that first encounter near the pinon trees, I was so thankful to have gotten away. I vowed never to let my guard down, never to be so distracted by food, or fun, or whatever, that I would place myself in such a vulnerable position. I do not know why I got away, why it let me get away, but I instructed the others, all the Ruminators, to be ever vigilant. But even so, even though I tried to let everyone know that they had to be careful, I had another, and much, much worse encounter with the creature... And that is why I want to ask you a serious favor. We need a protector; we need for you to let Candy stay here with the Ruminators."

Just then, Nougat came back in, followed by another small goat, this one a golden colored male. He was walking on all fours and carrying a bag of pretzels in his mouth. Removing the bag he said excitedly, "Gramma, excuse me! I was up top, you know, getting these snacks for the humans when I was almost spotted! A human drove up in a machine! A woman, I believe. I just had time to leap behind a boulder and run away before she saw me!"

116

"Mom!" exclaimed Marsha banishing all thought of the request that Salizar had just made. "That must be our mother. Oh, she'll be so worried, we left the walkie-talkie behind! We've got to go back up. She'll be so frightened. I mean, since Dad went missing last fall, having us disappear too would totally freak her out."

"Oh dear, thank you Nugget, for the information and the food, too. Humans, allow me to introduce my grandson Nugget. He is Nougat's twin brother... Yes, you kids must go to your mother. We will show you the way out, of course. We will help you in whatever way we can," said Salizar, trying not to be upset about the poor timing. Just when she was asking for their protector...

5 In the Mountain

"Well, good thing for brightly colored camping gear... If Marsha hadn't insisted on buying that ridiculously hot pink back pack, I never would have seen where the kids had hiked off too. Oh great, well, here's the walkie talkie, but where are those kids? Good thing I came along to scare that, whatever it was, from eating all their food or Shawn would've instantly starved when they got back. Mar-sha! Shawn! Phi-lo! Where are those kids? Hmm. I may as well walk around and see if I can find them..." Trudy switched on the two-way radio and put it back on the rock where she had found it in case the kids should come back while she was out looking for them. Then, shading her eyes with her hand and wishing she had brought a hat, she began to walk up the hill looking at the ground for footprints. It wasn't far to the place where the cave in had occurred, and when Trudy saw it she became frightened. She could tell it was newly opened earth, and could also see the teens' footprints leading up to it. Trudy quickly got down on her hands and knees and called down into the open earth. She couldn't see a bottom to the hole. In fact, the hole seemed to go off at a very steep slant rather than straight down. She leant over further and called again, feeling foolish for thinking that they fell down such a small hole. "If I just lean in a little more..." she thought, calling their names, "maybe I can see..." Suddenly the ground, more sand than substance, gave away from under her hands and in an instant she had toppled in, landing face first at the bottom of some sort of cave after skidding, sliding, and falling down the steeply sloping tunnel.

"Oh great. Well, now you'd better hope they are down here, you foolish woman," she said aloud to herself. Standing up and dusting herself off, she could make out the hole that had been her entrance into this underground chamber some distance above her head. Standing on her tip toes, she could almost reach the edge, but try as she might, her fingers couldn't get anywhere near a decent grip. The tunnel that she had fallen down seemed to be a one way deal unless she could find something big to stand on, or someone to give her a boost. "Shawn!" she hollered. "Mar-shaaa! Philooo! Can-deee!" Trudy sat down hard on her bottom to have a think about her ridiculous predicament when she heard a small quavering voice call out from the darkness.

"Hello lady, do not be afraid, you are safe, all will be well."

"Oh, thank goodness, someone is down here. Who are you? Better yet, where are you? Sure is dark down here. Did you happen to see three teenagers, a girl and two boys? Say, can you give me a boost out of here?"

"Alas, I am not able to get you out the way you got in," came the odd voice, " but yes, I have seen the children and they are safe. Follow me and I will lead you to them."

"Okay, I'll follow you gladly if you can lead me to the kids, but I can't follow you if I can't see you. Where are you? Haven't you got some sort of light? A match, anything?" Trudy searched her pockets, knowing that the only things she would find were the truck keys and a tube of chapstick. "I can't even see a passage way..."

"Pardon me, lady. My name is Sage. I do have a light; I will switch on my lamp. But first, I want to warn you... Please do not be frightened at the sight of me. I am not who you are expecting."

"Believe me, I wasn't expecting to meet anyone down in this or any other hole. At least not today!" said Trudy, thinking how strange it was that she was underground talking to what sounded like a little old lady.

Sage took a deep breath and switched on her little lamp, holding it up high. In the glow, Trudy saw for the first time the face that belonged to the quavering little voice and she couldn't quite match them up in her head. There, before her, stood a small, plump, brown goat with a black muzzle and black ears. It was standing upright on its back legs and it was holding up a lantern, a gently swinging little lantern, in what appeared to be its... hand?

"Wha-why, okay, Sh-Shawn, are you playing a trick? Kids? Come out now, very funny!" Trudy laughed nervously. "Very, very..." She couldn't finish her sentence. This really was a goat standing right in front of her, not six feet away! A real live, nope, not a puppet, not a hologram, a real live goat!

"I assure you, Ma'am, this is no joke, and there is nothing to fear," said the odd little goat. "I know where your offspring are. If you will kindly follow me, I will take you to them."

Speechlessly, Trudy began to follow the little goat with the human feet and hands. "I must have hit my head harder than I realized," she thought, running her hand through her hair, feeling for a bump.

***

The teens were preparing to leave their new friend Salizar, and her twin grandkids, Nugget and Nougat. Although the three of them, and Candy too, were having a fantastic adventure and they didn't really want to leave, they also didn't want Trudy to worry when she found all of their camping gear, but didn't find them. It was time for them to go back to the surface. Salizar had agreed to show them the way out. "We have several entrances to the cave. The place where the cave-in occurred is near one of the entrances. We will take you there," she said.

Shawn was wondering just how he was going to ask Salizar for the gold bars, and Marsha was pulling straw from out of the dog's furry coat, when into the sleeping chamber came a plump brown and black nanny goat. Sage bowed her greeting in that way of the Ruminators, and then she stepped aside to admit a new guest. Joyful exclamations ensued as Shawn and Marsha hugged their mother, with Philo and the goats looking on and smiling. Shawn couldn't resist the opportunity to make light of the odd situation by saying, "Funny meeting you here, Mom!" and the group all laughed and sat down once again in the straw.

They talked easily, back and forth, filling each other in on all the events that had transpired in the hours since the teens had seen Trudy. Marsha told her mother about how they fell in, omitting the part about the fool's gold, and Trudy told them all about her visit with SaraJane the lost and found Chi-Chi.

Sage was suddenly reminded of her own son, asleep in another chamber, as she looked on at the happy scene of a Trudy reuniting with her children. "Oh," she said, excusing herself, "it is time for me to wake my son. He protects the herd, and it will soon be his turn. I would love to stay and talk with you all, but a mother's duty comes first. Basher will be so happy to meet you!" Trudy expressed her gratitude at being found and safely led to the teens, and Sage bowed once more and left the happy group.

Trudy took a deep breath and gazed around the chamber with a strange look on her face. "I-I'm not sure what to say about all this! I mean, it sure is funny meeting you all here, and especially with your new friends. I'm hoping there is a reasonable explanation. That, um, little nanny goat who very kindly led me here to you, Sage? She filled me in a bit on the situation, but I have to admit that I'm in some major state of disbelief. I fell in a hole and I think I've hit my head and I might even be hoping that I'm actually in a coma at the Presbyterian Hospital up in Albuquerque," said Trudy.

The teens all laughed and nodded. "Yep, we've all entertained that idea too! Mom, I'm not even sure at this point what a reasonable explanation would sound like... But it looks like we really all did fall into a cave inhabited by a group of thinking, talking, thumb possessing, pardon the expression, goats!" said Marsha. "This is Salizar, she is the matriarch of this group. They call themselves the Ruminators, because of how they chew things over... how they think about things. She has been telling us stories about their history. And now that you are here, Mom, we can stay and listen to more of Salizar's stories about life under Ladron Peak!" She looked hopefully at her mother and added, "If that's okay?"

Salizar interrupted. "Marsha, you are all most welcome to stay as long as you like. Ladron Peak is not ours, and we don't really inhabit this cave, my dear. I mean, we don't actually live here. We are just here mining for our mineral salt lick."

"That's what I saw you doing when we first came into that big cave," observed Shawn.

"Yes, that's right. We travel here to your mountain for our lick. We Ruminators move around a lot. We don't actually live in any one place anymore. After my father and his friend Gizmo first heard about the chupacabra from the ranchers, the Ruminators were understandably frightened to stay and they left the hills near the area of white and headed south. There they found a great system of caves. There were many places to hide from humans, and many were the caves full of salts. Above ground they found fields of nut trees and many different types of delicious browsing shrubs. Life was good, almost perfect. It was there that I was born and there that I kidded my own offspring. My childhood there was wonderful, as was the childhood of my daughter, Primrose. There was time to play and time to spend in the sun. We almost forgot about the hot wind that wiped out most of our herd and changed us forever. We almost forgot all about the ranchers' tales of monsters. Almost. But then something happened. A new something. A bad something. And we decided it was time to move the Ruminators again. This time, we would travel north." Salizar paused, remembering, and hanging her head.

Marsha reached out a hand and stroked the fur on Salizar's neck. "Oh, I'm sorry, I didn't mean to pet you like you were an animal!" she apologized.

"That's all right, we are all animals, and we all need petting. I am sure even humans do. Sometimes memories make me sad and it's nice that you wanted to comfort me," she said.

Trudy spoke up. "The longer you live, the more memories you have. Some good, some sad... Best not to have regrets, but..." Trudy was thinking about Frank again. She seemed to be making a day of it. "Oh, gosh, I didn't mean to get so philosophical... must've really hit my head hard. Do you want to tell us what happened? I mean, did I hear you right? You did say chupacabra, did you not?"

"Yes, Trudy, I did. Chupacabra." As she said the word again, the elderly goat shuddered. "But not just that. Listen and I'll tell you what happened. I am the keeper of the stories, and I am duty bound to pass them on to all who would listen. Remember, we can not read or write. Yet. And so all of our history is oral. It needs to be told to be kept alive. And so... after we left the area of the chupacabra we had a good long stretch of an easy existence. But the Ruminators' new troubles began just over ten years ago when the WIPP came."

"The whip? What, you mean people were trying to enslave you, to beat you?" said Philo, with his knitted brow showing great concern. "Did people see you? Were you discovered down south?"

"It wasn't that people discovered us, but that we discovered people. People came into our home, into our caves! One day a strange board appeared, standing near our shelter in an area where we frequently came and went. It was a sign, with words we could not read. When I say WIPP, I am not talking about that thing that cruel masters use to beat animals, I am saying W-

I-P-P." Salizar carefully named each letter as she said it. "We heard workers talking and we learned that the markings on the board were letters; initials that stood for Waste Isolation Pilot Project. We did not know what any of that meant, not at first, all we knew was that our wonderful meadows were being invaded by men with heavy equipment, with road building equipment and big diggers. When we learned what the sign was announcing... when we learned what the men in earth movers had planned for our home... It was tragic. We listened carefully to the men, hiding around dark corners and eavesdropping to learn why they were underground.

The men with the WIPP were not mining; they were not there to take something from the earth, they were there to put something in it. The men planned to excavate our caves and fill them with more of that poison. Again, that is what the 'W' stands for – Waste. And not just any kind of waste, but nuclear waste. They said it was like the bombs, like the hot wind, but also not like the bombs. We did not fully understand, but we understood enough to know that humans were going to bury this stuff, this nuclear waste, about a mile underground in the salt and that it was enough like the bombs to give people the same kind of sickness. They were going to dig up our very floors where we laid our heads at night, the floors where we gave birth to our kids, and they were going to fill the earth with more of that radiation that had killed members of our ancestral herd..." Here Salizar's voice trailed off. She obviously was having a difficult time going over these events.

"I hope you don't mind if I interrupt," said Trudy. I understand from what little bit Sage told me that you are a byproduct of the nuclear weapons testing that went on at the Trinity site in the 1940's. Is that correct?" Salizar nodded. Trudy continued, "I'm not sure of the mechanics though. I guess the term 'testing' is somewhat of a misnomer for what went on there. But I gather that some of your herd became more intelligent creatures with human hands and feet and some of you died?"

"Simply put, yes" said Salizar. "We do not understand the mechanics either, but some of our ancestral herd died after a horrible sickness, while those who were not yet born came out as you see us. That is why we were so frightened when we heard what the men with the big equipment had planned for our new home in the caves. We did not know which of these outcomes might be the result. Or if there could be some other outcome entirely. We did not want to take the risk. The barrels they were burying contained the same kind of poison that was in the hot wind that killed our ancestors. Naturally, we knew we needed to get out of there."

"Gosh, what a hard time you guys have had!" said Shawn. "So you moved the Ruminators north. I hate to ask, but had you forgotten about the chupacabra?"

"We did not exactly forget, but there were barriers to the south. The men with the big diggers... And we did not want to stray far from the river, and so we went north."

Philo put his hand to his chin in a thoughtful pose. "And that it how you had your second encounter with the creature you say is the chupacabra."

"Yes," said Salizar sadly. "That is how."

6   Encounter

Once again Salizar got up and walked out of the chamber, excusing herself politely and returning after a few moments. Then she settled down in the straw without explanation and continued her story. "Yes, well, as I said, we don't live here under your mountain, we don't really live anywhere now... Not just because of the WIPP, although that is what made the Ruminators move away from our beautiful home in the south, but mostly because of what those ranchers were talking about..." Salizar paused to shudder. Marsha was sure that in spite of her fur, Salizar's face began to look pale. "It was because of my second encounter with the chupacabra."

Salizar then turned to look at the twins, Nugget and Nougat. "My dear grandbabies, could you two please go and fetch those shiny yellow bricks that we found on the mountain? Our guests will be leaving soon, and they were searching for them. I believe they are in the chamber where we keep the tools." The twin goats got up, bowed to their grandmother and wordlessly exited the chamber.

"I asked them to leave, not only to fetch the gold bars for you, but also because the next tale I have to tell is a very sad one that involves their mother..." Salizar paused to swallow hard. Then she said, with her clouded eyes shining, "...my daughter, Primrose."

***

It was a beautiful night, with the air still warm from the sun, and the darkness was cut into long shadows by an almost full moon. Spring was just underway and the usual daily winds had died down with the setting of the sun. It was the time of year in the hills around Socorro when the mesquite bushes with their long thorns began to sprout tender green leaves. Primrose and her two young kids were just preparing to leave the protection of their underground hiding spot to go above ground and begin sampling the spring treat.

"Okay, Momma's going to go out first. You two stay here until I call you. Don't worry, I won't be eating all the best buds, I'm just making sure that the coast is clear. You both know what Grandmother says, 'Better safe than sorry... look before you leap... act in haste repent at leisure... be on the safe side...' I'm sure I've forgotten some of her favorite safety idioms! But kids, I'm sure you get the message! Just wait here, be patient, and don't fight!"

Nougat and Nugget looked at each other and rolled their eyes. Recently the two young kids had started practicing their head-butting maneuvers, typical for goats their age, but annoying to their mothers. They were very close, and enjoyed playing with each other, but what they enjoyed most was sparring with one another. Nougat was forever trying to find some way to rankle Nugget into starting something physical. As their mother stealthily headed outside to check for predators, Nougat carelessly commented (in a calculated sort of way) that Nugget was always getting her into trouble with Mom.

"Am not, Nougat!" declared her brother. "You always start everything!"

"Yeah, and I always finish it too!" she laughed.

Nugget responded in the way that Nougat had planned for, by lowering his head and aiming his newly budding horns straight at his sister's skull when they heard a terrible cry come from just beyond the mouth of the cave. Without a thought to the lessons of their grandmother the twins charged out into the open where a terrible sight met their eyes. A strange and awful creature had a hold of their mother, its jaws clenched around her neck. Blood was running through Primrose's fur and her eyes were wild with terror. Nugget and Nougat charged forward and the creature looked up at them and snarled, showing its long horrible teeth but without losing its grip on their mother's throat. Primrose managed to garble her own mother's name, "Salizar!" along with the word "Go!" and the twins knew that she meant for them to leave the area and get help.

As hard as it was for the twins, they did as they were told, running as fast as their calloused, but tender, human like feet would carry them. They found Salizar napping in the sleeping chamber. "Hurry! Gramma! Momma's being attacked! Up top! Follow us!" they shouted. Salizar roused and quickly got to her feet, wordlessly following the twins back to the spot where they had left their mother.

"You both wait here!" commanded Salizar when they got to the cave's exit, and they knew from her tone that she meant it. She herself took no precautions at all, but bolted out into the open. In an instant she saw the body of her only daughter, lying on its side, and drained of all life. Thinking only of her beloved Primrose, Salizar sank to her knees to better embrace her daughter's body. She lifted Primrose's head into her lap, seeing the horrible wounds on her neck and feeling the lifeless weight of her. She cradled her head, nuzzling and feeling for breath, but knowing it was of no use. Primrose was gone. This thing in Salizar's lap was not Primrose, it was just the body she had left behind, drained of all blood. Salizar picked up the lifeless form and carried it back underground; back to Salizar's waiting motherless grandchildren.

***

"It's time for the night shift, Basher. Rise and shine little Ruminator." Sage spoke in a softly sweet voice. She was always gentle when trying to wake her only son from sleep. They didn't called him Basher for nothing. She had originally named her son Justin, but when his horns started to grow in, so did his

132

temperament. Not that he was prone to anger particularly, just that he was quick to react in any situation and always ready to butt his head into any trouble. Well suited for his job as a sort of security guard for the group. He patrolled the third shift, which was the most active time for predators in the desert. The Ruminators didn't usually have much trouble as long as they stayed below ground, but night time forays out of the tunnels could be dangerous, and it was Basher's job to patrol the known exits and entrances of their underground hideaway, making sure that there were no accidental interlopers or that herd members who for some reason wanted a moonlit stroll were in no danger.

"Mo-om", moaned Basher, "I don't know why you still persist in calling me your *little* anything! I'm about twice as big as you!" Basher tried to hide his face in the straw in an effort to return to sleep.

"Yes, you are, my delicious shrub, which is why I always try to waken you gently, so as not to get the wrong end of your horns for my trouble!" Sage gave her son a good-natured tousle between his tough horns and grinned. "Come on big boy! Time for duty!"

"Thanks, Mom, I like that better. Call me Big Boy anytime!" Laughing and rubbing the sleep from his eyes with his calloused hands, Basher used his horns to tidy his straw bedding up into a pile in the corner.

"Basher, I've got some news for you. Now, don't get alarmed, but while you were sleeping, some humans paid us a visit! Four humans to be exact, and very kind ones! They are no threat. Zero. And they have a dog with them! Down here, underground! I have just left them. They are all with Salizar in one of the large sleeping chambers. Perhaps you will get a chance to meet them during your shift."

"Wow, Mom, that sure would be great. Any chance they'll give us their dog? We have long dreamed of having a canine protector! Humans! And a dog! Imagine!" Face beaming with the news, Basher headed out into the tunnels to begin his night shift of providing security for the herd. "See ya later, Mom," he said merrily over his shoulder.

***

"So you see," said Salizar, "it was the chupacabra that got my daughter. That beast was responsible for killing her. The twins saw enough of the creature in the full moon's light to describe accurately the same creature that the ranchers had described and the creature I had seen with the jackrabbit. And so, the Ruminators live nowhere now. We run, we hide, we do not lead a proper life, being in fear of that... thing."

"It's so sad, so dreadful to think of! Those poor kids!" Trudy imagined leaving her own children. She thought of Frank, yet again, this time wondering how he could have left Marsha and Shawn. Poor Primrose, poor Nugget, poor Nougat, poor Salizar. It was almost too sad to contemplate. But then a light went on.

Trudy remembered. The detail, the piece of the puzzle that had been out of reach. It didn't make sense, not yet, but it had to be significant, it had to fit somehow... "Frank saw one. A chupacabra. In our yard. I didn't think about it until just now, but the day before Frank disappeared, he said he saw a chupacabra lurking around the chicken coop."

"Oh Mom, are you serious? Dad was probably pulling your leg!" said Marsha.

"Actually, that's what I thought. I thought that it was just one of his jokes. I figured that he was trying to scare me so that when I went out to feed the chickens or something, he'd throw a handful of hay at me to freak me out. You know your Dad..." Trudy paused and looked thoughtful. "But oddly, he wasn't being like that. He really did sound serious. I'm just now putting the pieces together."

"You mean to say that a chupacabra was in your yard?" asked Salizar. "I understand from the children that you live near here, near this mountain?"

"Yes, just across the river, across the Rio Puerco. We own five acres surrounded by a lot of nothing. About seven or eight months ago, my husband said he saw what he claimed to be a chupacabra trying to get into our chicken coop, but he said that he'd somehow scared it off. I didn't believe him, but he was unusually insistent. We never did straighten out the story because the next day, Frank disappeared."

Book Three - Frank

1 Sentry At The Entry

With the windows open Frank could easily smell the sack containing the strange dead animal that was in the bed of his pickup truck. Although he had only stopped briefly to look into the bag and hoist it into the truck, it took some driving for Frank to get in sight of the van that had dropped the special parcel. They both had started out driving on the one paved road that was on the west side of the highway, but the road was paved for only a short distance past the cattle guard and RV Park, less than a mile in fact. After crossing over an old iron bridge that spanned the Rio Puerco, the road continued, bumping along, alternating gravel with some deep pits of sand.

Frank knew that it ultimately wound back to some ranches and past a ghost town or two as it circled the base of Ladron Peak. He assumed from the government plates on the van that they were probably heading to the Wildlife Research Unit that was tucked somewhere back in there amongst all the nothing. That made sense, that they would be transporting the creature somewhere where they could do some research on it; perhaps an autopsy, DNA test, that sort of thing. It was odd though, that the zoology community at large hadn't been called in to look at this specimen before they took it to the restricted area of the Wildlife Unit. Frank thought that they'd at least notify the folks at the Albuquerque Biopark.

Perhaps it was because it was only very recently discovered. Hadn't Frank himself spied this animal in his yard only yesterday? Maybe this was the same one he'd seen. But he hadn't noticed quite as much of a stench coming from the animal that he had seen in his yard; this smelly critter in the sack may have been dead for longer than a day. Also, Frank didn't recall the animal by the chicken coop looking quite as terrifying and ferocious as this thing did either. Frank had scared that thing off easily. This guy looked a bit tougher. This creature certainly looked like it would put up a fight. Except that it was dead... "Well," said Frank to himself, "Maybe this isn't the one I saw. Maybe that means there are more than one of these, um, 'chupacabras' around. I bet those guys in the van would like to hear about the one I saw!"

***

The white van passed through a secluded area wooded with salt cedar and juniper trees and stopped at the guard house on the other side. The trees hid a pretty impressive security fence, and the guard house with a lone sentry inside was really all the protection they needed in this remote part of New Mexico. The driver of the van leaned out the window and spoke quickly to the man inside. "Looks like we got him. But boy, you should've seen! Unreal. Such a hard thing to kill! But we planted the bait, too. Our timing was spot on. Look out, here he comes."

Frank was following the van in his pickup as it made a sharp turn into the wooded area, and was startled at the sight of a guard house manned by what appeared to be an armed US soldier on the other side. "Wow, I knew this place was restricted, but I didn't think it was this restricted," said Frank to the frowning guard standing in front of the little hut.

The soldier told Frank to turn off his engine and then demanded to see his credentials, and he frowned even further when Frank joked that he didn't have anything other than his zoo pass. Frank tried to explain about the sack that had fallen out of the van. but the guard didn't seem to be getting the gist of his story.

He kept looking toward the group of buildings in the distance as though he was expecting someone.

"And you didn't touch the sack? You just left it where it was?" asked the distracted soldier. "I'll send for someone to go and get it, you can wait right here, sir," said the soldier.

Frank couldn't help but notice that the soldier had his revolver out of its holster and was holding it in his right hand. "No, I touched it, I mean, I have it, I mean, can you put that gun away? You're making me nervous," said Frank. "I have the sack in my truck, can't you smell it? Look, I'm just trying to return it. Sure I looked inside, I mean it stinks like dirty diapers and I didn't want to waste any of my expensive gas returning dirty diapers!"

The soldier was still holding the gun, ignoring Frank's request. He wasn't exactly pointing it at Frank, but he did look as though he was preparing for something to happen. He kept looking from Frank's face to the buildings and when no one came, he reached through the window of his little guard house and pressed a button on the intercom. Then he gestured for Frank to exit his vehicle. "Get out of the truck, sir," was all he said.

Frank complied, wondering why both he and the sentry were so nervous. He looked at the man's uniform for his name and rank, hoping to humanize the situation. "Look, Private... um... Trujillo... I've got the thing here, but I'd like to talk to someone in charge. I'm a biologist with the Albuquerque Biopark." When the guard looked perplexed, Frank filled him in. "You know, the zoo? Anyway, My name is Frank Maters... Dr. Maters... Ph.D. in zoology. I live in the area and I think I've seen one of these creatures roaming about my yard..."

Private Trujillo still looked nervous, but tried to regain his professional composure. "Sir, I need you to wait here, someone will be escorting you to the General."

"The General? I thought this place was for wildlife research? Why...what?" Frank stumbled to find words as he spied not one but two jeeps speeding towards them down the paved road. "Odd," he thought, just noticing the nicely surfaced road, "that the road is suddenly paved again! Our government dollars at work..." He shook his head as the trucks neared enough for him to see that each jeep held two men in army fatigues. Two soldiers in each jeep, one guy to drive the vehicle, and one, apparently, to hold the machine gun. "Whoa, okay guys," said Frank holding his hands in front of him with his palms facing the jeeps. "I just wanted to return this sack of road kill..."

2 Basement

"Try to do a simple favor, and end up in a military prison! ...If that's where I am..." Frank looked around at the tiny room. It sure did look like a cell. The room was very small, a four by eight foot corner of a basement, with two exterior adobe walls and two interior cinder block walls. A single bare light bulb hung from the ceiling and there was one small window high up on the wall that was the only source of fresh air. The window was cracked open slightly and had some sort of safety glass, the kind with wire running through it. Frank wouldn't be able to crawl through it or see out of it even if he could reach it.

A soldier had come in, dragging a plastic bucket, a gallon jug of water, and an army cot. All the comforts of home. "What did I do?" Frank had demanded of the soldier. The uniformed man darted a look at Frank that said "don't ask questions," and left him alone, locking the heavy wooden door behind him.

Frank thought over the events that had placed him here. It seemed that the only thing he had done was to admit to looking at the thing in the bag. Okay, so he also admitted that he knew what it was, sort of. He admitted that he'd seen one just yesterday in his yard, and he admitted to being a zoologist too. Big deal. How could any of that be a problem for the military? And what was the military doing out here anyway? The guy in the jeep, the one in charge, Sergeant Wilson was it? He seemed, beneath his bluster, to be unsure as to what to do with Frank. Perhaps they were just holding him here for a short time in order to be "debriefed" by someone higher up, this General that they promised. A wildlife research place couldn't be expected to have many Generals on hand, so Frank imagined that he'd have some time to kill while they fetched one.

Frank had seen enough spy movies to know that's how things worked; the potential spy was left alone in a room to sweat it out while some officials stared at him through a two-way mirror. No mirror here though, just that tiny opaque window. Frank contemplated that those spy movies never did end well for the guy being held for interrogation. He hadn't seen even one film where the suspected spy got released to go back with the wife and kids. Of course, this wasn't a movie. No, obviously not, because in a movie, they'd never let the spy keep his cell phone! Frank dug in his pocket, amazed to find his phone right where he'd left it. He flipped it open, index finger at the ready to press the 'send' button, but his excitement at the thought of hearing Trudy's voice instantaneously melted when he saw the

142

screen. Up in the corner, where the signal strength would be displayed, there were zero bars. Zero. Naturally, there was no signal.

"Duh," he muttered to himself.

***

Sometime later, in what seemed like hours but was probably just forty-five minutes or so, Frank heard footsteps approaching the door. Frank stood up from the cot and spoke out. "Hey, any chance you're here to feed a guy? I missed my lunch." By way of reply, the door swung open and in walked a large doughy white man in an elaborately decorated set of army fatigues. Frank managed a smile and stuck out his hand. "The General, I suppose? Look, I wasn't doing anything, I…"

The man put out his palm, not for Frank to shake, but palm facing out, as a sign for him to stop talking. Even though he somewhat resembled a marshmallow man playing dress-up, Frank realized the uncertainty of this situation that he was in and resisted his usual temptation to make jokes to lighten the tension. Frank remained standing, but silent, merely waiting to see what this man was going to say.

"Well, a good Samaritan, I hear," said the man, with a grin crinkling up his fat cheeks. Frank couldn't read this guy. Fake smile? Real smile? No way to tell, so he stood quietly, trying not to react in any way. "Listen," said the man "we've looked into your story, your credentials, and it checks out. Local guy just happens to be a zoologist, just happens to find one of our 'specimens', just happens to return it and sees our operation here."

What this guy was saying was true, just a list of the facts, up until the 'operations' bit. What the heck did that mean? Frank tried to remain silent, but found the quantity of questions that had amassed in his head after his lengthy wait was too great. "Um, excuse me, but I'm not sure what you mean by operations. I've lived around here for a while, and I knew there was a wildlife research area out here, but I understood that you were working on hantavirus. You know, messing with those cute little rodents and their deadly diseases? That's what the common knowledge around the Biopark is. So as far as 'operations' go, I don't have a clue as to what you're talking about. I had no idea that the military was involved."

The man's smile changed, but was no less difficult to read in regard to its authenticity. "Look I haven't even introduced myself. I'm General Schwinger. And you are Frank Maters, Ph.D. Pardon me, Dr. Frank Maters, I should say." Here he stuck out his hand for Frank to shake. "Yes, hantavirus. Yes, that research happens here," he said dismissively. "But you should not have seen that creature that you saw. Seeing it on your property was bad enough. Connecting it to the military… Look, I'm going to be honest with you. And I'm going to tell you the reason why I'm being honest, and I'm going to tell you the reason why you are about to join us in our work." The General clasped his hands behind his back and switched his weight from his toes to his heels and back again. "You're a lucky man, Dr. Maters! You have been chosen to help advance your nation!" General Schwinger paused for Frank's reaction, wanting to size up what he considered to be the patriotism of the man who stood before him.

"Okeydokes," said Frank, instantly regretting the silly tone of his remark. This guy with all the stars and ribbons was really making Frank nervous and he didn't like this situation one bit nor did he like the idea of being 'chosen'. "Let me just ask one question... When can I get to the hardware store? I've got a roof to fix today."

General Schwinger frowned, an expression of displeasure that was easy to read. "Dr. Maters, forget your roof. Your roof is small potatoes compared to the security of this great nation."

Frank thought to himself that it wouldn't be a very great nation if everyone had leaky roofs.

***

Frank had a hard time believing the conversation that followed. According to this General Schwinger, the government had plans for a new kind of weapon. A biological weapon created by atomic energy. It reminded Frank of the plots of several other movies he had seen. Not spy movies this time, but monster movies. It reminded him of one film in particular that took place in the desert near a test site where the radiation created giant ants. Crazy stuff. "What was it called?" Frank asked himself.

THE RUMINATORS

"Oh, yeah, 'Them!' ...With an exclamation point, no less." But could the government actually be doing that? Creating atomic monsters? This wasn't some 1950s' monster movie, this was the twenty-first century!

According to the General, the US government was planning to use a creature mutated by radiation to disrupt the tribal areas of the Middle East by destroying their livestock. Frank thought that he must have heard this guy wrong. The government, our government, wanted to destroy the lives of simple nomadic people that relied on their camels and goats for everything? By attacking them with some mutant creature? Nuts! This guy said that the thing that Frank had seen in his yard was not really the chupacabra of local legend, but an escapee from the lab. A creation of Man's cruel folly. Not that those were the words Schwinger had used. Schwinger had called the creature the ultimate weapon of modern warfare, or something like that. Yikes.

Frank was stunned when the General practically ordered him to stay and work on perfecting the care and breeding of these creatures. A state of confusion had over taken Frank and the General had left him, still in this rotten little basement room, telling Frank to think it over. General Schwinger made the assumption that any good red-blooded American patriot would be proud to work on the project, and he tried to offer compensation in the form of a position with the US Fish and Wildlife Service, deciding what animals are put on the endangered list. He seemed to think that would appeal to

146

Frank. But he didn't offer the position exactly, none of what the General had said was very definite. On one hand, a powerful government job. On the other hand, the man had made it sound like Frank wasn't going to be leaving the facility anyway with what he now knew. It was all so veiled. Alternating vague rewards with even vaguer threats. Schwinger was very talented in his use of allusion, innuendo, and suggestion. Scary.

Frank sat down on the cot to think. What had that guy really said? What are the facts? Frank decided it was time to put away the confused dad who just wanted to fix his leaky roof and bring out the learned scientist. "Okay, this is what the General actually said: They're perfecting this thing. (Whoever they are.) The thing is a radiation mutated, blood sucking killer with a preference for small furry animals. It particularly likes goats, baby cows, dogs. (Yikes, better keep Candy inside!) The plan is to breed a bunch of them, come up with some sort of diet for them that doesn't involve goat herds (something like ChupaChow?), so that they can be transported into Iran (not in so many words) and Northern Africa (not in so many words) to destroy the lives of nomadic goat herders (again, not in so many words). That about sums it up, right?" Frank paused to nod to himself in agreement. "Yep, that's about the size of it. Not in so many words... And he wants me to help, 'cause, number one, I'm a whiz with weird animal diets and, number two, I just happened along? Okay, that makes no sense. Did they lure me here with that sack? With the chupacabra in my yard? Is this all a trap? Will they keep me here whether or not I help in their evil plan? And just where is the hidden camera? This has got to be a joke..."

3 Gidget

Autumn and winter had passed and spring was nearly over. Some distance outside Frank's basement cell window, outside the boundaries of the Wildlife Research Unit, a herd of goats was doing what herds of goats do on a warm afternoon: eating, sleeping, defecating, and basically making a contented amount of noises and smells. All of the goats in the herd were doing those things, except for one accidental tourist of an animal.

Gidget had been snooping around, above ground without permission or invite, when she stumbled upon the group of ordinary goats that were browsing, unattended by humans, in the salt cedar bosque. Gidget had always wanted to commune with the "regular folk" as she called them, and sensing the absence of humans, she approached the group.

She bowed in greeting, but receiving no bow in return, she commenced to speak informally. "Well, hey there, ancient ones! My name's Gidget. I'm with a tribe called the Ruminators and

I've been wondering about you folk! Mind if I ask you some questions? Ya know, about what it's like to be so, um, traditional?" The goats in the herd considered her with a glance, their eyes so much like hers. But something was missing in their gaze. "Hey, did you hear what I said? Don't you speak English?" demanded Gidget. "Or don't you speak at all?" The goats continued to stare blankly at her. They were not alarmed by her presence, nor were they startled by her weird feet or hands, or her unusual way of bleating. The ancient goats accepted her as a member of the herd, unconcerned about having to share food or space or mates.

"Why, you guys are dumb as posts!" Gidget cried. "I was told, but I didn't believe it! I mean, you look just like us, except for your extremities!" Laughing she added, "And my, don't your tiny feet look funny! ...But I can see in your eyes...you don't see me. I mean, you see, you see me, but you don't recognize that I am an individual, a clever thinking creature! Oh, I feel sorry for you! This is all you do? All you know? Too sad!"

Just then, behind Gidget's back came the voices of two men talking. They were coming closer through the trees and Gidget heard one of the men say "Hey, I swear I heard a woman's voice up here!"

"Oh, you've been away from your girlfriend for far too long! A woman's voice, out here? You must be missing your old lady!" the other man teased.

The first man replied with a deadpan laugh as they came upon the herd... "Ha, ha, ha. But seriously, it didn't sound anything like my Trixie. It was kind of shaky, you know, like some old lady. ...More like Trixie's grandma."

Both men laughed. "Oh you're hearing things! Nothing here but a bunch of goats. Phew, I can't believe how far they got... I sure am glad we found 'em, or else we might have become dinner! Let's get 'em back to the Unit. It's nearly time to feed the beasts!"

Gidget looked frantically around her. There was nowhere to run. She had been so caught up in her thoughts about these ancient dumb goats, thinking about their sad little lives, that she forgot the one thing that ancient creatures never forget: to be always wary for predators. Not that these humans dressed in green were behaving like predators... but she mustn't be caught by them! Mustn't let them see...

***

"Got 'em all back, did you?" asked the guard at the entrance. "You sure woulda been in a mess of trouble if you hadn't! Them critters gotta eat something and I for one sure would prefer that they eat goats. You know, the General seems so mad these days...and I don't mean angry...he'd just as soon feed us enlisted guys to those...things. I really don't know what the government is up to with this research..." The guard shook his head and looked nervously around him. "Hey, forget I said that. Seriously, you never heard me say anything. Just drive to the corral, unload the goats and make sure you latch that gate this time!"

The truck pulled forward, onto the paved road that led on towards the paddock. Gidget shivered in the back amongst the ancient goats. She had waited too long for just the right chance to runaway and had missed it, pushed instead into the back of the truck by the herd mentality of these dumb, crazy goats. "Gosh, move over you stupid beasts," she hissed under her breath. "Well," Gidget thought, "at least the shoving and pushing of these ignorant mammals kept my feet and hands hidden. Why are they so intent on complying with the humans? Don't these goats know what their fate will be?" Gidget pondered a life dedicated to the service of humans. The offering of their milk, their young and sometimes even their own flesh in exchange for food and water and shelter. Was it worth it? Gidget thought of her own mother and father, of her aunts and uncles and cousins and grandparents. "Imagine them being abused in that way! I guess it sometimes helps to be just a dumb animal if that's what will become of your friends and relations…"

After the goats were unloaded into the corral, a process during which all the jostling and pushing of the herd hid Gidget's special traits once again, Gidget lay on the ground in the shade of a small goat shed to survey the scene. She kept her hands and feet tucked beneath her body and breathed a sigh of relief. Luckily, no one had noticed the extra goat with the odd characteristics. She watched as the man closed the latch on the gate that the goats had not-so-kindly escorted her through. It looked simple enough to unlatch it. "I suppose that they don't bother to take extreme precautions with the gate, after all, these ancient ones don't possess thumbs, and therefore can't have my talents for escape!" she thought. "But I guess they got out once. Maybe they're not so dumb after all?"

Gidget knew that it would be best to wait until nightfall for her escape and she figured that she still had a few hours to wait, now that the days were so long. While she rested up for her long walk back to the Ruminators and their caves, she had a look around for any other possible exits, making sure that she took note of where any windows were located as well. She didn't want any humans to look outside tonight and witness her escape.

From her low vantage point in the shade, she could see two gates leading into the enclosure that she was in. The first gate was the one that she and the goats had entered through, and that gate led out into an open area where various jeeps and trucks were parked, including the truck that Gidget had ridden in. Gidget thought that this would be her most likely way out. The second gate led from the goat enclosure into another fenced in area that surrounded a large metal building. The sandy beige building had two doors that Gidget could see, but only skylights on the roof and no windows. That second gate was locked with a heavy chain and padlock. The fence that it went through was quite tall and was topped with coils of some very pointy looking wire. A third gate allowed access to that same building's enclosure from the open parking area. It too was heavily chained and padlocked.

Across the parking area was a large two story adobe structure. It looked old, but in good repair, like a renovated and amended ranchers' homestead. The adobe building had several windows that faced the goat enclosure, including a couple of small windows that were just a few inches above the level of the ground, but all the windows looked like they had some sort of curtains or blinds, so Gidget was not particularly worried about humans seeing her from there. There were a few more buildings, but they were all some distance away and Gidget thought that they posed no threat as long as she ran in the opposite direction, toward the juniper trees. "Escape should be a piece of cake," thought Gidget, adding to herself, "I wonder what cake is..."

***

In the basement room attached to one of those little low windows of the adobe farm house, Frank still languished. He had been there for what seemed like an eternity and nearly was. He had lost exact count, forgetting on some days to make marks on his makeshift calendar, but he approximated his stay at over seven months. "I'll sure have some story to tell when I get out of here," he told himself for the umpteenth time. "I've missed Thanksgiving, Christmas, Valentine's Day...even Marsha's birthday... I wonder what they think has become of me? I hope they don't think I'm dead. I hope they don't think I've run off..."

Frank sighed and cracked open a well worn copy of Orwell's Animal Farm, ironically the only decent book that the illiterates at this so-called research facility had managed to come up with when Frank pleaded for some entertainment. Frank had read it at least once a week since he had stopped cooperating with the powers that be. He had worked for a while trying to come up with a diet other than live mammals that would be acceptable to the mutant beasts. A packable food was needed so that the creatures could be transported covertly and used as a secret weapon. The explicit idea was to drop groups of these things into places where they would wreak havoc on the livestock of people too poor to influence world policies anyway. The plan was at once ridiculous and cruel minded.

But Frank suspected an even more sinisterly implicit plan. Though the General never said so, not in so many words, it seemed that his intention was to get those beasts to attack humans. Frank knew that the guy was tapping the soldiers for frequent blood donations and that he'd even gotten a couple of pints out of Frank before Frank refused. Perhaps this General was so much of an evil nut that he was trying to get the beasts to go for humans by giving them a taste for their blood. Heck, the man had even made jokes about it! He had posed the idea that wars could be fought using this new kind of biological weapon and no government could even be blamed. "What? Your country has been infested by chupacabras? That's too bad. Nope, we don't know how such a thing could have happened... Don't look at us..."

Frank just couldn't stomach being a part of it. How could the United States Government condone such a wild and nonsensical plan? And not only condone it, but foot the bill, as well? The laboratory and living quarters for the mutant creatures were state of the art. Nothing like it at the Biopark, surely, where zoologists and biologists worked to save endangered animals with captive breeding programs. Nope, this was expensive equipment, hidden in a remote prefab metal building for the exclusive purpose of tinkering with the DNA of a voracious carnivorous animal, one already mutated by nuclear radiation. The goal of all this great equipment wasn't to save or improve lives, but rather to fine tune and enhance the creatures' traits for murder and mayhem so that they could be used as weapons against innocents. Beyond crazy.

So here sat Frank in his little cell, uselessly waiting, hoping for the day when this insane plan, developed by this nut of a General, was somehow stopped and he could go home. Maybe someone would expose the project to the right-minded citizens of this country or maybe it would quietly run out of funding. "Either would be fine," he thought. But what Frank feared most was that someone in Washington would keep signing the checks and the project would continue working, developing monsters for warfare, and that Schwinger was just keeping him around to use as a test dummy. "They've erased me from my life, my family, my job, and whaddya bet that crazy General Schwinger plans to erase me from the planet... by feeding my fluids to those beasts..."

***

Gidget kept replaying the plan in her head, reassuring herself over and over that escape from the compound looked pretty simple. She merely needed to wait until nightfall and then unlatch the gate that led to the parking area and make a run for it using first the trucks, then the adobe building and finally some groups of trees for cover. She might even leave the gate unlatched behind her so that all of the ancients could escape as well! As Gidget pondered the wisdom of that idea, a human entered the goat enclosure and pulled on the horns of an old nanny goat that was lying down and chewing her cud. He led her to the gate that went to the enclosure around the prefab metal building, opened it using a key hanging from a chain on his belt, pushed the goat through and then locked the gate behind them. "Strange," thought Gidget, "that the gate through there is so heavily locked. Are they trying to keep the goats out?" The man led the goat into the building, this time pressing buttons on a security panel next to the door in order to gain access.

Gidget, curiosity getting the best of her, wanted to move closer to that building. She had plenty of time to kill until she could make her break for home and she thought she might as well use that time to learn what she could about this place and the people here. She reflected on her ride in the truck with the ancient ones and how exciting that would have been if she hadn't been so scared. The first Ruminator to ride in a human's vehicle! Something made her want to know what was going on in that building; maybe it would make for another great story to take back to her friends. A group of goats passing by provided her with the cover she needed and she walked, crouching down behind them, to get nearer. All of a sudden, the goats she was hiding behind stopped and stiffened as an awful noise came from out of the windowless metal structure.

Frank looked up from his book and flinched in pain as he heard the sounds coming through his tiny window. The horrible piercing squeal was the all-to-familiar sound of a goat in pain and fear as it was being offered to one of the mutant beasts held within the laboratory. "Sure, every thing's gotta eat," Frank shouted out loud, "but those monsters shouldn't even exist!"

4 Escape!

It seemed like an interminably long amount of time before darkness fell and the goat enclosure and surrounding compound quieted down for the night. After Gidget witnessed the horrible event of that afternoon, after she heard the terrifying sounds that issued from the metal building, Gidget was afraid. More afraid than she had ever been in her life. She hoped that no man would come into the enclosure and drag her towards the beige building before she could have her chance to flee. But at last the goats were quiet, their usual daytime bleats replaced by soft breathing sounds. No more trucks were driving in or out of the parking area, no more humans were out and about, no more men had entered the enclosure, no more goats had been led away.

Gidget noted that there did seem to be one solitary human patrolling the compound. She had seen the man with the shooting stick over his shoulder walk through the parking area three times this evening and was waiting to see if he came around again and if his walks were routinely spaced. Although the events of the day were making her anxious, Gidget knew that it was important to wait if her escape was to be a successful one, and so wait she did. Eventually it became clear to Gidget that the man with the gun was coming through the area as part of a regular route and that she should make her move right after his next pass.

Sadly, Gidget made the decision against rousing the herd of ancient ones. They all heard the horrible noise that came from the metal building and Gidget saw the ancient ones stiffen at the sound. They were all aware that the old nanny goat never returned. Whatever it was that had happened to that goat, it was frightening and terrible and she certainly didn't want it to happen to any of the others. Gidget felt devastated for not helping the other goats to escape, but she worried that having a whole herd of goats romping around in the dark would rouse all of the men in the compound, and she didn't want that either. That wouldn't save anyone from the poor nanny goat's fate, not even her. So just after the guard made his fifth walk through the parking area, Gidget crept quietly over to the gate, undid the latch, and slipped out. It was with huge pangs of sadness and regret that she re-latched the gate. "Maybe I can come back with support and set them free," she thought.

Gidget crossed the open parking area which contained just one vehicle at this late hour, planning to hug the building and go around its corner. Then it would be a short sprint to a stand of cottonwood trees and another short sprint into an area dotted with junipers. Just as she got to the side of the adobe house, the man on patrol suddenly returned, shining his flashlight back and forth on the ground and muttering quietly, "Darn, darn, darn, darn..." He was looking down, and hadn't seen the little white goat slip into the shadows.

"Oh no!" thought Gidget. "The guy has lost something! He's dropped a vital something or other. Oh, I sure hope he finds it quickly!" The soldier stopped moving his flashlight and bent over to pick something up off the ground. He moved the object towards his face and flicked it into flame, lighting his waiting cigarette. He gave a sigh of satisfaction and then turned on his heels and walked back in the direction that he had come. "Phew!" said Gidget. "That was close!" She clapped a hand over her mouth, silently chastising herself for stupidly speaking out loud. She was just about to continue with her escape plans when a hurried whisper came from the tiny basement window.

"Hey, is somebody out there? Damsel in distress here..." joked Frank, standing on his cot in an effort to get closer to the window. He had woken up from his recurring dream about roof repair, feeling stifled in the oppressive little basement room and had been trying to get some fresh air through the tiny gap in the window when he heard Gidget's voice.

Startled at the unexpected sound of the human male's voice, Gidget replied before she could think. "Um, bleat, sorry, did you say damsel?"

"Yeah, I said damsel. Did you just bleat?" Frank chuckled, a rare sound for him lately. "Hey! The evil warlord has me trapped in the tower and won't let me go! I think he plans to feed me to his dragon in order to save the kingdom!" This was not the first time Frank had uttered this ridiculous statement. A few weeks back, Frank had spoken to the very soldier that was on patrol this evening. The soldier was sheltering from the ubiquitous New Mexico spring winds near the adobe wall to facilitate the lighting of his cigarette. Frank had laughingly told him that "real soldiers don't smoke on patrol," which earned him a mild grunt in reply. The soldier then took his lighted cigarette and sauntered away, saying nothing more. This time, Frank was surprised to hear a woman's voice. He hadn't been aware of any women being in the compound. "Hello? Lady?"

Gidget was very excited to talk with Frank. She had never spoken with a real live human before! She had eavesdropped on them, and had now ridden in an actual truck with two of them, but she'd never had a back and forth conversation. But this was so not the time! Here she was in the process of escaping and she really had to leave; what if she were discovered? Oh, but this was too delicious, too great of an opportunity to miss! This human couldn't know that she was, well, what she was. Gidget thought, "He must be thinking that I am a human. Just like he is!" Out loud she said to Frank, "Um, my name's Gidget, but I think I'm the one in distress. I'm in the process of escaping here, and I really need to get a move on before someone spots me!"

"Honestly? Really? Gidget..." Frank was taken aback. "Like the surfer girl in the movies? I didn't know there were other folks prisoner here. Makes sense. That General Schwinger is a monster! Look, you can't leave me here. You've got to help me get out! We've both got to get away, and get the word out! Let people know what's going on at this supposed research facility. That creature that they are breeding... I know what it can do, and not just to those poor goats over there... that madman has a horrible plan to use it as a weapon! We've got to stop him! You've got to help me escape!"

Gidget was flustered. This was not part of her plan. She needed to get back home. What this man was asking of her was way over her head. Gidget couldn't even save those goats. She knew that she wasn't equipped to help a human. But this man said that he wanted to stop whatever it was that they were doing to the goats. He has plans to put an end to whatever horror is happening in that building. Gidget reasoned that by helping this man, she could perhaps help to save the ancient ones too. She resolved to do what she could. She spoke to the window. "But how can I? I'm just a...I mean, what do you need me to do?"

Frank had it all figured out. He had dreamt of a chance like this for months. "Listen. Go around to the other side of the building. There's an unlocked door. There's supposed to be a guard at his desk, but he usually goes out for a smoke with the guy on sentry duty. Wait for him to go out, there's some trees you can hide in. And then slip in the building, get down to the basement and unlock my door."

It all sounded so simple the way the man laid it out. Except for the unlocking the door part. Gidget had never even opened a door or entered a building before. She especially wasn't sure about locked ones. "How do I do that?" questioned a doubtful Gidget. "How do I unlock a door?"

"Well, I'm not exactly sure..." said Frank, adding hopefully, "Maybe you'll find a key?"

Though Gidget was doubtful about the plan, she couldn't just leave this guy here. She already felt bad about abandoning the ancient ones, after hearing that horrible screaming bleat that the nanny goat had made earlier in the day. Whatever these humans were doing in the big metal building without windows, it wasn't good for goats and, if this guy was right, it wasn't good for anyone. But even if she did get inside and find a key, would she be able to use it? She thought again of the old nanny goat, picturing the man leading her off, holding her by her horns. And then she imagined that it was one of the Ruminators. "Okay", she said, "I'll try."

***

Gidget had to wait quite a while to see the guard leaving the building. It would soon be approaching morning and the nearly full moon was just setting, making long shadows of the trees. Gidget's light colored coat would surely stand out in the moonlight and so she was careful to wait in the shadows of a stand of cottonwoods while she observed the door. She came around the corner of the building just in time to see the parting of the guard and the sentry. Apparently they had just finished their smoke break and Gidget figured that she would have to wait for their next one.

The time passed slowly while she waited, giving Gidget plenty of time to weigh the pros and cons of rescuing, or at least of trying to rescue, this human stranger. The cons were beginning to weigh a bit heavier than the pros when the sentry finally came back around the far side of the building. He knocked twice on the door for the guard to come out and join him and then the two men ambled off in the direction of some vehicles, reaching into the open interior of a jeep and taking something out. Gidget waited while they walked further away, out of sight, before sprinting to the door of the adobe building. She reached up and tried the knob, only to find it locked. "Oh no!" she whispered aloud. She was sure that the man had said it would be unlocked. Then Gidget noticed that although the knob was locked, the guard had left a small stone jammed in the doorway, whether on purpose or through accident, she didn't have time to decide. Pulling the door open, she slipped inside and began to look for the way down to the basement and wondering what else the man would be wrong about.

Looking around her, Gidget wanted to examine everything she saw, but had no time to marvel at the human-made space in which she found herself. She walked past the guard's desk and turned down a hallway to her left, and there they were, the stairs heading down. And not only the stairs, but hanging on the wall near them was a pegboard with a single set of keys dangling from it. Could it be? Gidget was relieved to think that she had made the right decision to rescue this guy; it was turning out to be so simple. The only problem was that the keys were hung up high on the wall, at human height, not at little goat height. "But that's no problem for me!" thought Gidget. "I can climb like a goat, and I can also grab a chair like a human! I may never have used a key before, but I saw that man do it just today. I can do this!" She went back to the guard's desk, grabbed his chair and heaved it over to the top of the stairs. It was a heavy, old government issue office chair circa 1975, but she managed it fine by pushing with both her hands and her head, and then she hopped up on it, grabbed the key from the pegboard and flew down the stairs as fast as possible. "This must be the door!" she exclaimed, as she began rapping on the only visible closed door in the basement. "Hello, man, I'm here! And I've got the key!"

Frank was ecstatic. He was finally going to get out of this basement and get the opportunity to tell the world about those creatures and the General's plot. Not to mention the opportunity to reunite with his family. "Hurry," he said, "we've got to get away before he comes back!" Frank heard her fumble with the key, trying several times to get it in the lock. "Are you sure you've got the right key?" he asked. Finally, Frank heard the key slide into the lock and heard it unlatch. Frank joyfully pushed open the heavy wooden door and standing there, holding the key in what appeared to be its hand, with what appeared to be a broad smile on its face was... "A goat?!" said a shocked Frank.

"No time to explain!" Gidget said. "We've got to go!" Frank hung his head, sad to find that this was only another dream. He must still be asleep in his cot, dreaming that the ghost of one of the creature's unlucky victims had come to rescue him from this dreadful place. He was about to lie back down on the little cot and go back to sleep when he suddenly heard a noise from upstairs, and the little white goat beckoned again for him to get a move on. The guard had returned from his smoke and had found that his chair was missing from behind his desk. The man looked over at the stairwell and saw his chair standing there, nowhere near where he had left it. Looking from the chair to his desk and back again he said, "What the...?"

The guard's voice came down the stairwell to Frank's ears, finally rousing him from his stupor. "Oh, nuts," he said, "we gotta go!" and picking up the little goat and tucking her under his arm, he barreled up the stairs. At the same moment, the guard was approaching the stairs to retrieve his chair and in the split second that he noticed the keys were missing from the peg board, a man carrying a small white goat knocked both him and the chair over and ran out the door of the farmhouse just as the sun was coming up.

5 The Hunt

Trudy stretched and looked around the cave at her son, daughter, nephew and dog soundly sleeping on their bed of straw. Trudy had intended to camp with them on the mountain last night, roasting marshmallows around a campfire and sleeping under the stars. Instead, they had all slept inside of Ladron Peak, in a deep, dark, underground cave. The matriarch of the Ruminators had sent a couple of goats "up top" as they called it, to retrieve some of the snacks that Trudy had left in a cooler at the kids' campsite. The Ruminators knew the tunnels and all of the various exits and entrances well, and the kids wanted to stay and talk with Salizar and her grandkids just a little while longer. The Ruminators seemed very happy to have the human house guests, though Trudy gathered that Salizar was still trying, gently but firmly, to get Marsha to give up her pet dog, Candy.

Trudy had no idea what time it was, she usually didn't wear a watch and her phone's battery was dead. "It sure is hard to know what time of day it is down here," she thought, although some light was making its way down into the space through the narrow channels in the ceiling. Trudy thought that she might as well let the kids sleep as long as they liked. They had all had quite an exciting adventure since their cousin Philo came to visit. He had inspired her kids to go on the hunt for stolen Wells Fargo gold and they had all experienced unimaginable events, and had made some unusual new friends. Trudy couldn't wait to tell her sister Janice what a fabulous kid she and Bert had. "In the meantime," thought Trudy leaning back in the straw, "I'm going to enjoy the peace and quiet..."

***

Frank ran as fast as he could with Gidget under his arm. He headed first for the juniper trees, hoping for some sort of cover. He would have preferred to run in the direction of home, but as the sun had fully risen over the horizon and the desert was nothing but wide open spaces between here and there, his instincts told him to head for the trees, the bosque, the foothills. Frank ran like that, with Gidget unceremoniously jiggling about under his arm for some time, before he remembered that he was even carrying the little goat that had rescued him by unlocking a door. He also suddenly remembered that she had spoken to him.

"Hey, bleat, um, Man, um, I think I know of a good hiding place! Head north... toward the foothills of that mountain. If we can keep hidden in the bosque... bleaah... it's sort of far, but I know where there are some good tunnels that we can hide in!"

"Tunnels?" panted Frank. "What kind of goat goes underground?" Then, pausing to think a minute about this extraordinary creature that he held under his arm he said "Okay, so that's why I've never encountered your species before. You are some sort of rare, tunnel dwelling sentient goat. Makes sense? ...Not."

"Look, bleaah, there is an explanation. But first we need to get away from that dreadful place and those awful humans. Are you sure you disagree with what they are doing, bleat, with what they are doing to the ancient ones? Aren't all of you humans the same?"

"I don't know what you mean when you say ancient ones, but I certainly do disagree with what those men are doing back there. The only thing I want to do now is to get back to my family and stop whatever plans the government has for those horrible creatures!" Frank was panting heavily now, out of shape for having been stuck in that crummy little basement room for so long. "Do you think it's okay if we rest for a bit? I mean, do you think the soldiers are behind us?"

Gidget replied, still jiggling around with the man's arm uncomfortably squeezing her udder. "I think it would be safe if we rested for a few minutes, but I know there is a road somewhat near here. We should remain alert. I am terribly sorry that I cannot return the favor and carry you. We certainly are covering more ground using your long human legs!" Frank put the little goat down and flopped flat on his back in the shade of a salt cedar tree and closed his eyes. Gidget stayed standing, stretching each odd little leg in turn and introducing herself. "I'm Gidget, but they call me Gadget sometimes. Some of the others tease me because I am so interested in the things that people use. Like that key back there that I used to unlock your door. I have never used one before, but I've seen padlocks on gates and I've seen ranchers use them. Ha, wait till I tell the others! Looks like it pays to be interested in human gadgets!"

Frank got up on one elbow and looked at the odd creature. He was trying not to think too hard about the details of his escape from his basement cell back at the compound by this weird talking goat. He didn't dare question what she meant by 'the others'. "I'm certainly glad you happened along with your knowledge of keys and locks. Thank you, thank you so much. I'm Frank, by the way. That name really fits you. More so than Gidget, I mean. Mind if I use it? Mind if I call you Gadget?" he asked. "Yep, Gadget, you'll never know just how happy I am that you figured out how to use that key!"

"Me too," she said. "I'll be known as Gadget, from now on!"

While Frank rested in the shade, Gadget told him a bit about how she had come to be captured and taken to the compound

172

with the 'ordinary' goats. She told Frank that the goats had been browsing somewhere near where they now were and the soldiers had no trouble finding them and putting them in their truck. "Jeez, why didn't you say so!" said Frank. "We'd better be off then!" And the odd pair continued on, with Frank carrying Gadget as before.

***

"What?!" shouted General Schwinger. He was awake in less than no time. The men said he slept with both eyes open, which wasn't exactly true, but the man was a light sleeper, always on the alert. But just because he was easy to awaken, it still didn't turn it into a pleasant task for the private entrusted with it. Rather, waking the General was like waking a light sleeping bear in the middle of its winter hibernation. The risk was that any human alarm clock might lose a limb. "Soldier, what do you mean 'the prisoner has escaped'? What prisoner exactly?" he growled.

"Beg pardon sir, but I'm referring to the prisoner that was in the basement of the farmhouse. The uncooperative zoologist. Somehow he managed to escape. The guard on duty says he heard noises like someone was moving about downstairs and he went to the stairwell to check on it. Suddenly the guy comes barreling up the stairs carrying a goat, shoves him aside and runs out of the building."

"He took a goat did he?" The General let out a small snort of a laugh as he stood up and began to pull on the pants of his uniform. "I knew he was a bit of a weak link in the food chain. Soft hearted for goats!? Ha! ...Who've we got trailing him? I hope that guard saw which way he went. We can't have this guy out and about telling tall tales about our operations here. Not yet at least. We've got to get that Ph.D. bleeding heart goat lover back." The General looked thoughtful for a moment and sat down heavily on his bed. He punched the mattress on either side of him with his fists, letting his pants drop to his ankles as he did so. Then a broad grin spread across his doughy face. Speaking aloud to himself as though there wasn't another person in the room he said, "What a great opportunity! Yesss... Hmm, a test! Perfect!" He stood up again and addressed the man who was still standing at attention in front of him, protocol commanding that he ignore the location of the General's pants. "Soldier, why don't you let me finish getting dressed and we'll join the hunt!"

***

It was nearly high noon when they reached the destination that Gadget had talked about. They were in the foothills of Ladron Peak, among some rugged looking rocks. The sun was bright and hot and there wasn't a cloud in sight. Frank said aloud with a huge grin on his face, "Great weather to be free in! Don't cha think so, Gadget?"

Gadget looked at him with eyes wide-open in surprise as she heard what sounded like a truck's engine, some small distance away. The little goat squirmed in Frank's arms, trying to get down. "Quickly! Put me down and get in that hole!" whispered Gadget in an urgent tone.

He tried to place Gadget on the ground gently, but the wriggling goat landed harder than Frank intended. "Oops, sorry, Gadget," he said. Then looking at the hole in the ground that she was ordering him, a fully grown man, to climb into, Frank frowned. "Are you kidding? I'll never fit down there! Plus, look, I can just about see my house from here," he said, standing on his toes and shading his eyes from the solstice sun. Looking back towards Gadget and the hole he said sadly, "It still looks so far away…"

"Quickly Frank, you will fit, you will! Trust me! It's only small for a very short way. Then it widens out. I know it's not like your house across the river, but it's pretty much where I call home these days. Quick, Frank, no time! Don't you hear the truck?"

Gadget jumped down the small hole. Frank had little time to think. After they had burst out of the stairwell and trampled down the night guard, it probably didn't take long for the guard to raise the alarm. Thank goodness that the soldiers who patrolled the compound at night were a generally useless bunch. But they weren't so useless that they couldn't wake up General Schwinger. And with that madman on their tail, Frank had better find a good hiding place. They had already been out in the open for too long. And now Frank's human ears could hear the same truck that Gadget heard. "I can't believe I'm following the advice of a talking goat. But, she's a talking goat that has done what no man seemed able or willing to do..." thought Frank gratefully. "Okay, this is definitely not time to think. I must trust the goat!" And with that, Frank dove head first into the hole, surprised to land unharmed on his stomach at the weird feet of his new friend.

"Come on!" she said urgently. "We can't stand around here! This tunnel will provide us with a great hiding spot, but I know I heard a vehicle! The more distance we put between us and them, the better! C'mon, Frank, get up, I'll take you to our leader."

"Your leader? You did say there are more of you. Hey, what are you anyway? Alien goats from another planet? Or were you manufactured by those mad soldier scientists too?" Frank was trying to stay serious, but as was usually the case with Frank, he couldn't resist a giggle. The situation was serious, even deadly serious in light of the General's insane plan and the fact that he was probably following them, but Frank's relief at being out of that basement and seeing his home, even from miles away, was huge, making him giddy. And it didn't help that he was taking to a little white goat with the silly name of Gidget. Or Gadget. Or whatever.

Gadget rose up, somewhat less awkwardly than Frank would have thought possible onto her hind legs. She gestured with her hands, palms up and open. "I get that you're still shocked. And probably very tired and hungry too, but trust me, I know about hiding. My kind has been on the run for a long time. We need to get a move on." She put her hands on her hips and gave Frank what looked like a smirk. "Or can't you walk and talk at the same time?"

"Hey, a goat with a smart mouth! Gadget, I like you, you remind me of home...and a certain member of my family... I assume you know the way?" Smiling, Frank switched to a robotic alien voice. "Take me to your leader!" he said, gesturing for the goat to proceed. "Ladies first, of course!" Gadget trotted off down the dark tunnel with rock walls and a sandy floor. Frank laughed and shook his head to clear away some welcome but unwise silliness and dutifully followed.

***

The soldiers were standing well back from the crates perched on the flatbed truck, even though there were only small wet breathing noises and quiet rustling sounds coming from the creatures inside, sounds that could arguably be made by a group of slumbering puppies. Back at the compound, the soldiers had loaded the steel cages onto the truck bed with the aid of a winch. But the men were acutely aware that they didn't have any of that sort of equipment out here on this dirt track in the high desert. Any unloading of the cages would have to be done by hand. Taking them down off of the truck wouldn't be so bad. The cages were heavy, but had comfortable handles welded onto sheets of solid steel, with only small air holes drilled in the sides for ventilation. No chance for any snarling, snapping, biting, bloodsucking jaws to get through. But it would be a different story when the soldiers were commanded to unload the contents of the cages... The young enlisted men were trying hard not to think about that.

Hat and aviator sunglasses protecting him from the late afternoon sun, General Schwinger stood, hands clasped behind his back, legs wide apart, aiming for the appearance of a fierce and commanding attitude as he surveyed the progress of the man hunt. He was waiting for confirmation that the zoologist had been located. The young Sergeant who stood nervously next to him spoke. "Yes, Sir, we saw him head for the foothills. He was definitely still holding that goat for some reason. The man's footprints lead to this area. We think he may have gone to ground." General Schwinger thought it was appropriate that Sergeant Wilson had used a hunting term, for the hunt was soon to begin.

6 Reunited

Frank and Gadget had slowed to a trot as they got farther away from the entrance of the tunnel and closer to where the Ruminators would be mining their salt. The two new friends had opportunity to talk, and Frank was able to clear away some of his confusion. "So Gadget, what were you doing hanging out with those 'ordinary' goats in the first place? Did you get caught, um, borrowing people stuff? You said you like humans' gadgets; were you on a hunting trip?"

"No, bleat, I was stupidly trying to make friends with the ancient ones. Wrong end of the food chain, I'm afraid."

"Oh-kay" Frank drew out the word, not really understanding what she meant. "So you are some sort of newfangled goat? And by ancient ones you mean…?"

"Yes, my herd is rather new. From the mid 20th century. By ancient ones, I mean regular, ordinary, run-of-the-mill goats. The traditional kind that you are used to. It's a long story, and I don't mind telling you, but later. We are close to getting to where the herd is located and where we will be able to get something to drink and sit down and talk without all this gasping for breath. Let me just say for now that we are a product of your nuclear age, apparently much like those dreadful creatures..."

After a few hundred yards they came to a tunnel that looked more like a man made hallway. The walls were straight and appeared to be hewn out of the rock, and there were timbers framing the entrance. The floor was strewn with sand as before. Looking down, Frank could see numerous oddly long footprints in the soft sand. He was amused to see the many hand prints left by the Ruminators as well, as though he was taking a stroll on a beach frequented by people who often walked on their hands. "Ha," he laughed, "I see that some of your kind have discovered the joy of hiking boots. Not so fun to go barefoot in the desert, huh?"

"Oh no, I don't know any of the Ruminators who have managed to 'borrow' any shoes. Believe me, I have tried. When I was a kid I wondered why our hands looked like human hands, but our feet did not look like human feet. You see, I had never seen a human with bare feet before, and so I thought humans' feet were all high-heeled and pointy-toed. I now know that what I had seen were people wearing cowboy boots. But one day I discovered by chance a shoe that had been abandoned near a dirt road. The shoe fit me rather well in spite of my long back feet. It was great protection from stones and thorns! I searched

180

and searched for its mate, but never found it. ...Eventually it fell apart." Gadget looked downcast, remembering fondly her old shoe. "I have never had another one since. Sometimes I have seen shoes tied in pairs and slung over telephone wires and I wonder how anyone could be so flamboyantly careless. Sometimes the Ruminators walk on four legs, sometimes on two, but try as I might, I can't get those shoes down from the wires... I sure would love to own some shoes!" Gadget scanned the sandy floor and saw what Frank had been talking about. "Hey, you are right! I do see shoe prints! Who among us could have been so lucky to have found a complete pair?"

They slowed their pace to a walk now, their genial conversation calming their nerves after all the excitement of the chase. Frank relaxed his shoulders, feeling that although he was about to meet more of these talking goats, at least he was out of that basement and closer to getting back home to his family. Then he would try his hardest to put a stop to the General and his so-called research center. Gadget looked over her shoulder at Frank. She was walking, almost strolling, on all fours now. Clearly she felt more relaxed too. "Salizar must be in the sleeping chamber. I can hear her voice up ahead. Won't she be surprised to see a human in these tunnels! I hope she will not be angry..."

Gadget stepped through the passageway and let out a loud bleating gasp. "Oh my!" she exclaimed, "It appears we have lots of human visitors!" She bowed before Salizar as a sign of respect for the elder matriarch and stammered "S-S-Salizar, I was worried you might be angry with me! I have brought a human into our midst, a necessary risk! Apparently, you have had to take a similar risk? I-I-bleat!" Gadget took a deep calming breath and spoke into the passage way behind her. "Please, do come in." Turning back to those gathered in the chamber, both humans and Ruminators, she bowed once more and said, "Salizar, new human friends, I should like you to meet... Frank."

All eyes, human and goat alike were on Gadget as she spoke and all eyes grew wide as Frank entered the chamber. He had to lower his head to navigate the rather small entry way and when he raised his face to the sight of his family, sitting cross-legged on the straw covered floor of an underground cave, Frank could not believe his eyes. For so long he had wanted to be back with his family, and here they were, gathered around an elderly goat. Frank rubbed his tired eyes and smiled broadly at Trudy. He was certainly thinner and paler than when his family had last seen him, but was still undeniably Dr. Frank Maters, Ph.D., husband and father. They all sat in stunned silence for a moment, each trying to process what they were seeing. Could it be true? It was Marsha who was first to reconcile her eyes with her heart, and she lunged for Frank's neck and uttered the name she hadn't used since she was a toddler. "Daddy," she whispered.

***

"I see no reason to delay any longer. We shall release the

182

Laura Wacha

creature into the cave as a supreme test of my project! It is interesting that the prisoner should have chosen to take a goat into the cave with him. Its scent may well aid our beast in locating and attacking its prey!" The General looked frighteningly amused. "Though I cannot see how our biologist friend would benefit by having a goat as a companion. The goat will only serve as an appetizer to the main course!"

Sergeant Wilson held his tongue. He was certain that the General had to be acting on his own, without any approval from Washington. There was no way that any sane government official would condone such a plan! "We have created a monster," he thought, "and this mad man wants to turn it on the human race. God help that man down in the cave. With these blood thirsty beasts after him, he cannot stand a chance!" The Sergeant shook his head as if to clear away the cobwebs. He could not hold his tongue any longer; he had to act. Now. Wilson squared his shoulders in an effort to stand bravely up to General Schwinger. "No! General, I cannot stand by and let this happen! This is not what I nor any of these other men signed up for! I promised to defend our country, not destroy it!" Wilson reached for his service revolver and drew it out of its holster and aimed it at the General's heart. "I'll not let you kill that man! I'll not let you turn this monstrous creature into a weapon against mankind! I'll not let you…"

The end of the Sergeant's sentence became a garbled shout as the General quickly drew his gun and shot the man in the hand,

183

causing him to drop his weapon and cry out in pain. One of the soldiers standing nearby kicked the Sergeant's gun away and leveled his own at the officer's head. Sergeant Wilson sank to the ground, clutching his bloodied and mangled mess of a hand.

"So, you're not going to...what was that again, Sergeant?" asked the General, voice like ice. "You should not have wasted so much time with your noble little speech. Here's a tip. If you ever get another opportunity, shoot first, talk later." Then he smiled broadly and laughed with a wicked snort as the man on the ground looked up at him with hatred and agony alternating on his face. Schwinger turned away from Wilson and addressed the other men present. He still held the pistol in his hand as he spoke, casually waving it at the men as though he was conducting a band. "Well, now we have our next guinea pig. How thoughtful of the Sergeant to volunteer, right men? He obviously blew a fuse and became sadly suicidal! No one could stop him, right?" Schwinger looked at the man on the ground. "Well, Sergeant, you just might be more of a challenge for our creations. I mean, I'm sure that biologist won't put up much of a fight, being all pale and skinny like he is....and probably not much blood in him either! But the Sergeant here is in great shape. Except for that hand. Tell you what. I'll play fair. We'll give you a sporting chance." The General then addressed one of the men. "Private Chavez, take the Sergeant back to Maters' old cell. Get the medics to give him a Band-Aid or something. We'll let him heal up a bit. Replenish his blood supply before..."

He didn't finish the sentence but turned his attention to the crates sitting on the back of the truck. Suddenly the look on his face changed from sinister amusement to sinister business. He turned to the men that were there to attend to the cages and instructed them to make sure that the beasts went down into the cave a.s.a.p., well before sundown. "We want to make sure they've got plenty of time. And make doubly sure that the radio transmitters are on and that those things get their dinner! I want to know as soon as the job is done!" The General looked at the Sergeant still curled up on the ground. "Take this man away first, will you? We don't want his blood all over the place when we release the creature. The Sergeant isn't their target. Yet." Looking directly into Wilson's eyes he said, "Oh, and don't worry about the paperwork, Sergeant Wilson; I'll take care of it."

***

"Well, Dad, you did always say that you wanted us to be more adventurous! How's this for adventure? We fell down the rabbit hole yesterday, and we've been hanging out in Wonderland ever since!" said Shawn who was grinning ear to ear. "Oh and hey, do you remember cousin Philo? He's what brought us over here. Hard to believe, but Philo got Marsha and me to come out on a camping trip looking for the lost gold of Ladron Peak!"

Marsha chimed in. "Philo is awesome Dad! We've had a great time with him. And now that you're back, well, the fun will just exponentially increase!"

"Listen to my Marsha! Have you been studying your math vocabulary while I've been gone? Exponentially? Pretty good!" teased Frank. "Hey, smart girl, I missed your birthday, I'll make it up to you, promise." Frank made motions with his index finger of crossing his heart and gave Marsha a warm smile.

Leaning up against the rock wall, Trudy sat quietly, watching while her children and husband exchanged affectionate pats and hugs and good-natured comments, impossibly trying to take up where they had left off, as if he were just returning from an exceptionally long trip to the hardware store where he had completely forgotten to buy those nails. Frank was giving Candy a belly rub with Marsha still hanging from his neck when Trudy asked, "Excuse me, my family, but I for one would like to know… Frank, just where have you been all this time? Would you mind filling in some gaps for us?"

Frank looked at Trudy wondering where to begin. Taking a deep breath he said, "You won't believe it, but I've never been more than ten miles away. You know that nature reserve back behind Ladron? The one that's closed to the public? The place where they are supposedly doing research on the hantavirus? Well, I've been there all this time. I think they set me up. ...I'm pretty sure they did. The Army that is. Or someone pretending to be them. It's somewhat confusing, because their motives... or methods..." Frank couldn't complete the thought.

"Anyway, they're not exactly studying rodents back there. They're developing this horrible creature. Breeding these monsters... To use as a weapon of sorts. And they actually wanted me to look after them! To tend to the needs of the ungodly things, and help make them more, um, user friendly." Frank saw the look on his wife's face go from confusion to disbelief to fear. "But of course I refused and so they threw me in a basement. I've been there the whole time. Until this little goat saved me. You wouldn't believe it! Guys, this here is Gadget, well, Gidget really, like the surfer girl from the movies. She's a magnificently terrific, um, person. I'd still be in that basement if it wasn't for her!"

"Yeah, but Frank, bleat, don't forget. Those men may be after us. Well, after you, really," reminded Gadget. "You said that you didn't think they'd just let you walk away! Not with what you know..."

"Oh, Gadget, you're right! Thanks for bringing me back down to earth... Or under it," he chuckled. "I'm so happy to see you all again; so happy to be out of that basement! But, yeah, I've got a lot of work to do! The guy in charge, this lardy creep, General Schwinger! I can't believe our government is behind a man like that. The creature he has created is dangerous. And his plan is unreal... to introduce a species like that?! Well, beyond the immediate risks of having your livestock or even your people eaten by this thing, there are the long term damages to the balance of nature. This thing is not natural. No offense to our friends the Ruminators; from what Gadget said, I guess you guys aren't natural either. But the Ruminators are at the totally opposite end of the danger spectrum. These engineered beasts are voracious predators; horribly wasteful eating machines. They suck the blood of a mammal and leave the remains. They need far too many mammals to supply even one of them with enough blood." Frank paused and swallowed hard. "The General had all the soldiers on the base donating their blood. Just to feed these things. And I think also to give them a taste for humans..."

He could see the looks of horror and incomprehension mixed together on his family's faces. "I know this is a lot to grasp, but with something like this out and about, we can forget about foreign species like the saltcedars and tumbleweeds. We can stop worrying about the survival of the silvery minnow and the spotted owl. We will be demoted so far down the food chain, it won't be funny. We'll be no safer than our little goat friends here! No safer than the jackrabbits out in the desert and a lot less efficient about replenishing our species!"

"Oh Frank," said Trudy breathing a contented sigh, "at the risk of sounding like I'm glad to hear this news, I need to tell you how happy I am that you had a really good reason for not coming home that afternoon! I just knew there had to be some reason why you left us. I mean, some real reason." Trudy smiled weakly, realizing that she was sounding selfish. "Of course, we'll help in whatever way we can. Tell us, exactly who is after you? What's this General's name again? Something funny sounding... Schwinger, was it?" Trudy laughed nervously just as her husband's face took on an expression of horror at the sound of the evil man's name.

7 Let Loose

The two men stood rigidly at attention, right hands held up in salute, left hands holding the release cables which were attached to the gates of the steel cages. They both glanced nervously at their commanding officer as he climbed into his jeep and told the driver to head back to the Research Unit compound. A cloud of dust followed the jeep as it drove away, but the soldiers relaxed their shoulders only slightly as they put their right arms down. Apparently, their orders were to be issued remotely, via radio. When the orders came, the soldiers were to pull on the cables and head for higher ground. Although these things had insatiable appetites for blood, the researchers hadn't quite gotten their development perfected as far as climbing skills went. The men had been instructed to jump up on the back of the flatbed. No one in charge seemed to care that the truck wouldn't really be high enough should the creatures turn on them. Even a medium sized dog could jump up there with no trouble. But the enlisted men of the Research

Unit were well used to taking orders from General Schwinger, used to following the kind of orders that sounded as though they might have been designed to include potentially tragic outcomes. They had seen the creatures hidden inside the steel boxes and they had seen what they could do. Releasing that kind of horror into the wilds of New Mexico, even in this rather remote spot, gave each of the men a sick feeling in the pit of his stomach. As soldiers, they knew better than to question any General, and as men, they were keenly aware of the kind of horror that this particular officer was capable of, regardless of his rank.

Halfway down the dirt track that would take the jeep back to the compound, the General still appeared to be enjoying the anticipation. The soldier driving the jeep looked at the man, hoping to see some evidence of humanity in light of the order he was about to give. Could he actually be looking forward to this? "Gentlemen, release the beasts!" he said into the two-way radio in a casually dramatic fashion, as though he were an announcer starting a greyhound race. The order was given, there was no turning back. The two soldiers didn't look at one another, each afraid of showing the fear and doubt they were trying to keep inside. Instead, they did as commanded, counting to three and pulling on the release cables. Private Downing jumped back quickly to climb on to the flatbed but Private Trujillo managed to catch the toe of his boot on the edge of one of the large tire's lug nuts. He fell down hard in the ochre colored dust and scrambled for a hold on the tire at his back.

Downing shouted for Trujillo to grab his hand, reaching over the side of the truck in a moment of panic and terror as the creatures emerged from their crates.

"Please don't let those things turn back towards us," thought Private Trujillo, frozen with terror. "Please..."

Almost as though it could read the young soldier's mind, the first creature to emerge from its crate turned its hungry black eyes toward the man on the ground and showed its sharp yellow teeth in a wicked grin. It blinked and squinted from the bright sun and then tilted its head, almost as though considering Trujillo's request. Private Trujillo lay stock still against the tire, sweat instantly flowing from his every pore, waiting for the attack that he knew was coming. But the creature just snarled at the soldier and squinted its eyes before turning away and slithering down into the darkness of the hole in the ground as was intended; down into the hole where the escaped biologist had fled with the little goat.

Both of the soldiers would have been easy pickings for either of the beasts. If they had wanted to, one of them could have lunged at Private Trujillo while the other leapt up on the truck where Private Downing was with no trouble. Instead, each creature slunk out of its cage, apparently less interested in a meal of soldiers' blood than in escaping the bright sunlight. Their huge black eyes, more adapted for hunting in the dark of night, squinted even in the waning late afternoon sun and Trujillo and Downing watched in relief as the greasy creatures with their sharp yellow fangs and spiny backbones slunk down underground into the cool darkness.

The two enlisted men inhaled deeply, realizing they had each been holding their breath. Then they indulged in a few moments to recover, to let their blood pressure and pulse rates come down a point or two while General Schwinger demanded their report on the radio. Checking their equipment, Downing responded to the General. "Sir, we've got a good signal on the beasts. They're moving rapidly in a northerly direction..."

"Good" said the General. "I'm going back to my quarters. Let me know when the beasts stop long enough to do some damage."

Downing and Trujillo monitored radio signals from the creatures as commanded, each silently wondering what the plan was for their recapture when the dreadful job was finished.

***

Frank didn't want to frighten his family anymore than was necessary, but their elation at seeing him again was making it difficult for Frank to convince them of the immediate gravity of the situation. "I know this all sounds like a fantasy, especially in light of being here with our new friends the Ruminators, but we've got to act..."

Salizar had been listening quietly to Frank's story and other than introducing herself and some of the other members of the herd she hadn't said anything. Now she felt that she had to speak up. "Frank," she said, "we know these creatures that you are speaking of. We know them as the chupacabra and I am filling in the gaps of our combined histories. I think we have a similar origin, the Ruminators and the chupacabras, but from what you say, these men are engineering, or reengineering, these creatures for warfare? Is that right?"

"Yes, I thought at first that they were just going to use the creatures to attack livestock. Sorry, I don't mean just... But I thought at first that the idea was to try and disrupt the lives of goat herders in the Middle East or something; to get the tribes to fight amongst themselves. I mean, that's bad enough. But I think it's even worse than that. I think that they are developing these things to terrorize humans. That they want to set 'em loose in populations where wide spread death is desired without US presence. I'm totally convinced that this General Schwinger isn't dealing with a full deck, so maybe he's not even doing all this with any real authorization. I overheard a guard one night, talking outside my window. He said that the entire project had been totally defunded, imagine... because of ethical problems! ...Ya think?"

"So what should we do, Frank?" asked Trudy, "Call the authorities? Or we could go straight to the press with your story. I've still got some contacts at the Journal. We'll make sure this information about the so-called Wildlife Research Unit is front page news!"

"I think the press, yeah. I mean, I've had quite a bit of time to think about this down in that basement. But first, I want to get you guys away from Bernardo. I'm actually glad that you guys are down here and not at the house... These guys know where I live, so I think we need to get away, a.s.a.p., and then go straight to the press. Tell the story. I'm not sure the local authorities would believe us, or even be clean for that matter. After all, someone is turning a major blind eye. Anyway, I think we should get started right away!" Frank began to stand up, which wasn't easy with the limited amount of head room.

"Oh Daddy, don't you want to rest for a bit? You and Gadget have been through a lot! It sounds like you were up all night and running all day! I think it's already getting near sundown. You must be tired, hungry, thirsty? And we've missed you so much! Can't we sit and talk some more?" pleaded Marsha.

Shawn joked weakly, "Look, Dad, pretzels and water. Your favorite..."

Taking a deep drink from the offered bowl of water, Frank passed it to his new friend Gadget. He then grabbed a handful of pretzels and said, "True, Gadget and I have been running most of the day. But I did get some sleep last night before Gadget happened along. Sure, a nap would be nice, but guys, I think we'd better go now. I mean right now. I'm fine, running on adrenaline at this point. I don't trust that General not to..." Frank's voice trailed off.

"Not to what, Uncle Frank?" asked Philo.

Frank seemed disinclined to finish the thought. "Well, I just think we should get some distance between us and them. We need to get ourselves back to civilization. I am sooo looking forward to being among actual civilized people behaving in an actually civilized manner! You good creatures have no idea..." Frank laughed in spite of himself. He had been in that basement for so long, it felt like the whole world had gone bonkers because bonkers was all that he had been able to see. He was incredibly relieved to find that the people he loved were still living their ordinary daily lives. Looking around at the mix of humans and goats sitting on beds of straw in an underground cave he thought, "Well, sort of ordinary..." Turning to his friend Gadget he asked, "We're under Ladron Peak, aren't we? What is the easiest way out of here? In the direction of the Rio Puerco."

Salizar replied for Gadget, "I can show you to where Trudy has left the vehicle; near the children's campsite. It's not too far from here. Follow me."

8 The Tunnels

"Time to get up, Basher. Rise and shine, Big Boy." Sage once again spoke to her son using her waking up voice, but was careful this evening not to call him her 'little' anything.

"Mo-om", Basher moaned, rubbing his eyes and replaying the same scenario that mother and son went through every night.

"Yes, I know, son, waking up is hard. But you'll be happy to hear that the humans are still with us. I know you were disappointed that you didn't meet them last night, due to them being asleep," said a sympathetic Sage. "So you have another chance. Plus, I have heard that your friend Gidget brought back another one, if you can believe it. A man this time! From one of her crazy adventures. It seems that we are getting quite the collection of humans! Some might say we were becoming infested with them!"

***

The five humans and their dog followed along behind Salizar and Gadget as they led the way through the darkened tunnels. Philo still had his tiny windup flashlight with its occasional whirring sound and Gadget carried a small battery powered lantern. The Ruminators were aware of a tunnel that would bring them all above ground near to where the teenagers had first set up their campsite. It would therefore put them all within easy reach of Trudy's pickup truck.

Nugget and Nougat quietly followed some small distance behind. Their unspoken tactic was to make themselves as invisible as possible so that their grandmother wouldn't notice them. Salizar was forever trying to spoil their fun, usually in the name of safety or education or nutrition or something equally as dull. The twins thought that this outing just might qualify as educational, but they were having such a good time they worried that Salizar might think otherwise. Nougat was enjoying listening to the family of human beings and she didn't want the eavesdropping to end, even though the humans seemed to be having some pretty intense conversations. Nugget thought that the humans were so funny, with their hairless skin and weird eyes and they way they stood upright all the time.

After walking in single file through the tunnels for nearly three quarters of an hour, and sometimes having to crawl through some tight goat-sized spaces, the group was finally approaching the exit. Candy could smell the fresh air and was starting to feel playful, jumping from one member of the odd little group to the next. Salizar looked fondly upon the romping dog and she decided to try one last time to convince Marsha. "We really would be in your debt if you would consider leaving Candy with us," she said. "We have long thought that a canine would give the Ruminators some well-needed protection."

Marsha looked from her happy dog to the hopeful Salizar. "I'm sorry, Salizar, really I am. But I simply couldn't part with her. She is a member of our family, and I need her! ...Oh gee, I don't know why I didn't think of this before... Salizar! We'll have no trouble finding a protector for you! Humans are too often abandoning some wonderful dogs! The Valencia County animal humane takes in stray and abandoned dogs, and then adopts them out. I promise you that we will get the Ruminators a nice, big, strong, loving, protective dog of their own! As soon as we can."

At hearing this, Salizar beamed. "Oh, young Marsha, I knew the first time I saw you lavish affection on your canine that you were a special human. Was it only yesterday? ...Thank you, Marsha! Oh, thank you all!"

"Oh, nuts!" said Shawn stopping in his tracks, "Can you believe it? I forgot the gold bars! I gotta go back…"

"Are you kidding me, Shawn?" said Trudy and Philo simultaneously. Trudy continued talking alone. "Do you have to go back now? Can't we get them some other day?"

"Oh Aunt Trudy, it's the reason we came out here. Our mission won't be complete without..." Philo was interrupted when suddenly, a voice shouted from outside. "Halt! Who goes there!?" Instantly, Frank felt his stomach drop fearing that a soldier had been waiting for them at the campsite, until a laughing black goat put his horned head into the tunnel's entrance. Salizar practically jumped out of her skin, but Frank let out an audible sigh of relief.

"Basher!" Salizar shouted, "could you possibly not be such an alarmist all the time?!"

"Hey, it's my job!" Basher said with a grin. "But don't look now Salizar! You're being followed by a bunch of dangerous humans!"

"Basher, these people are our guests," said Salizar in a formal and reproachful tone. "We are just escorting them out of the tunnels and then they are leaving."

"Yeah, my Mom told me that we had human company! I hope you folks don't mind, but I was nosing around your campsite. Making sure the coast was clear for you. Looks good. Except maybe for a visit by a marauding raccoon! Something seems to have eaten all your food! Nothing left but empty wrappers..."

"Oh, that was no raccoon, that was probably just Shawn," quipped Marsha, getting an affirming giggle from her mother. "I'm sure he had finished most of our food stuffs before we fell into your cave!"

"No, some of that was me," said an apologetic Nougat. "I'm sorry, but I was up here yesterday looking for something to feed you...and I admit it, maybe looking for a souvenir as well?" Nougat looked sorrowful, especially under his grandmother's reproachful look. "I'll return the item I took. I'm not even sure what it is. Some sort of little white bag with two red stripes around the opening. There were two of them and so I thought you wouldn't miss one..."

Philo laughed. "It sounds like you got one of my socks! Keep it. Wear it with my compliments! In fact, I'll give you the mate, too!"

"I, bleat, I guess I might have tasted a bit of your food too. Sorry if I made a mess." Nougat turned to look at Basher, who had now stepped down into the tunnel with the others. "Anyway, if I know you, Basher, you weren't worried so much about the welfare of their stuff, you were just waiting to catch a glimpse of the humans!"

"Well, great minds think alike, right Nougat? See, I did want to meet you... My mom told me a bit about our visitors, but not nearly enough. You've probably met enough of the Ruminators to know that we are all fascinated with humans. Perhaps we feel like kin?"

Turning to Trudy, Salizar told her that Basher's mother was Sage, the goat that had led her to their chamber after she had fallen into the sink hole. Then she turned to Basher and said,

"You are in luck, young buck. It seems the human Shawn has forgotten something. Could you possibly be a dear and take him back to the sleeping chamber to retrieve the gold bars? We don't want him getting lost. And while we wait, we can clean up the mess. Right, Nougat?"

Basher smiled and nodded. In spite of Salizar's proper manner, she always tried to indulge the younger goats of the herd, making sure that their curiosities were satisfied. "Sure, I'd be glad to take Shawn back. Ruminators' Security Systems at your service! Shall we?" Basher stood up on his back legs and made a slight bow, gesturing for Shawn to lead the way.

"Hey," laughed Shawn, "if you're providing security, shouldn't you go first?"

Philo interrupted the good-natured bantering between Shawn and the buck Basher. "Um, would you mind if I go with you guys? I'm pretty fast. Lickety-split!"

"I don't know, Basher," said Shawn slyly, "he's also the kind of guy who says things like 'lickety-split'!"

"Shawn, can you guys wait a minute?" said Frank, drawing his son aside and speaking in a lowered tone. "Shawn, would you talk to Basher about... you know, the creature. Just to give him a heads up. You know, make sure the Ruminators are on the alert."

"Sure Dad, I'll tell him. Look you sit down and have a rest and Philo and I will be back with the gold in no time. Lickety-split."

Frank laughed. It suddenly dawned on his tired brain what their errand was about and he asked quizzically, "Gold?" as the odd trio began jogging away with Philo's flashlight whirring.

Trudy called after them, her voice echoing back out of the tunnel. "It'll be dark soon, so please... Hurry back."

***

A few yards down the path, Basher turned back to Shawn and Philo, who were a short distance behind him. "Just checking to see if you're still there! Um, bleaah, sorry, I overheard your father tell you that you were to talk to me about something. Some creature? Some sort of security issue?"

"Yeah," said Philo looking to Shawn for his okay to deliver the message, "well, you see, Uncle Frank just escaped from a so-called research facility near here…"

"Escaped from?" interrupted Basher, stopping in his tracks.

"Yeah, that's right, Dad escaped from this military facility where they have been developing these killing machines…"

Basher's eyes took on a stunned look and his body instantly tensed as he interrupted again. "Killing machines? I am known for being easily alarmed, but the Ruminators are sadly experienced with some of the destruction caused by humans. Our history tells us of bombs that radiate unseen poison and dangerous waste materials buried within the earth herself. So tell me, what kind of threat is this new machine?"

"To begin with, it's not a machine at all. It's an animal," said Philo. "But it's not a natural creature, it is an engineered one. I hope you don't think that we're passing judgment on the Ruminators. We know you're not really natural creatures either. These other creatures that Uncle Frank has told us about were developed using that same unseen poison, that same radiation, that you are familiar with. But these animals have been perfected in a lab, solely for the purpose of destruction." Philo paused and looked introspective, as they continued their walk down the tunnel. "Created for destruction, perfected for killing, isn't it all a dreadful oxymoron?"

"It was Dad who said this beast is a killing machine. I think he called it that because it's a creature that kills and eats voraciously, almost for sport. Salizar told us that the Ruminators have encountered a chupacabra? Well, Dad thinks this thing is created out of that one. I mean, that the chupacabras of local legend are actually radiation mutated creatures like you, but that the things in the research facility have been made worse through genetic engineering... Sort of a Chupacabra 2.0. Dad says this creature is nearly indestructible and so he wanted us to warn you... 'Pack up the Ruminators and go,' he said."

Basher looked down at his hands as he walked along on all fours. "Salizar is the one who would make a decision like that.

But I will take up these concerns with her." He paused, standing still again. "But, bleat, I do not understand. Why would anyone create a creature like this? Don't they fear for their own safety?"

"Who knows?" said Shawn shaking his head. "Grown-ups do some pretty weird stuff. That dreadful oxymoron like Philo said. Create to destroy... Anyway, keep an eye out, will you Basher?"

***

Emerging from the cool darkness of the tunnel, Marsha and her parents breathed the fresh warm desert air for the first time in many hours. The sun was still up, although it would soon be disappearing behind the mountain. "Aah," said Marsha, "That sun feels good. Hey, today's the solstice, the longest day, beginning of summer."

"Yeah," said Frank, "we just need to clear up a few loose ends with those rat bags at the research center, and then we can start some serious summer vacation activity!"

Nougat pointed out the direction of the campsite, and the group proceeded over a small ridge, instantly seeing the bright yellow tents, now collapsed on the ground in the near distance. Candy ran ahead and was romping around happily, snuffling at the ground for bits of crumbs and kibble amidst a wide array of stuff when the others reached her. "Oh jeez," said Trudy, "willya look at this mess? Oh, but there's the truck! Oh happy day!"

Salizar looked at Nougat and Nugget who stood behind Gadget, both shyly grinning at their grandmother. "Well, my little goatlings, here's your chance to make yourselves useful. Why don't we get this place cleaned up while we wait for Shawn and Philo to return?"

Laura Wacha

9 Dead Ends

Shawn shifted the weight of the bag on his shoulder. "It sure is heavy," he said.

"Here, I can carry one, Shawn. My water bottle is empty anyway. I can use the holder and put one of the bars in it. Here, Basher, want a water bottle?"

"Sure, thanks! I'll add it to my collection! Hey, I know you're pressed for time and all, but we've got the gold and, well, would you mind if I showed you guys something? It's actually on our way back, just with one tiny detour," said Basher.

"What do you want to show us, Basher? Your collection?" asked Philo, trying to hide his amusement. The Ruminators loved human junk and Philo was reminded of a friend of his back in Chicago who loved to dumpster dive. "Can't wait to tell Kenny about his kindred spirits," he thought.

207

Basher beamed proudly. "Yeah, how did you guess? I've got some great stuff in my collection, but there's a couple of human artifacts that I can't figure out. I don't know what they could be for." Basher, for his part, would consider himself to be more like a museum curator than a dumpster diver. His love of human detritus was purely intellectual.

"Sure," replied Shawn, "we'll come look. I can help you out with identification. If there's one thing I'm good at, it's stuff."

The three of them made a few turns down some tunnels. Philo marveled at the underground system. "Wow, it's really quite intricate down here, isn't it? Did you guys make all of these passageways?"

"No, they were just here. Some natural, I guess, and a couple of the chambers were apparently hideouts for thieves and bandits. We actually found that gold down here, but we couldn't find any use for it," answered Basher.

"How come you didn't add the bars to your collection?" joked Shawn.

Basher replied, somewhat affronted, "What's their purpose? The gold bricks have no function, not even any moving parts! After all, I haven't got a rock collection!"

Just ahead of the trio in the darkened tunnel, Basher's ever alert ears picked up an unusual noise. His rectangular pupils widened to take in as much light as possible as he strained to see the source of the sound. "Shhh," he whispered back at the boys and held his hand out to quiet Philo and Shawn's laughter and stop them from continuing any further down the path. The three of them stood quietly, with the teens' ears straining to hear what Basher's already could. Suddenly the sound came into focus and Shawn and Philo could hear the strangely wet rattling noise too, bringing to mind the sound of a live diamondback encased in tub of jell-o.

The three of them each backed up a step as the strange noise got nearer. Then, emerging slowly slinking out of the darkness came the pointy snout of the snarling beast, its breath, heavy and hot, filling up the small space with a dreadful stench. Philo's tiny flashlight beam glinted dimly off the drooling yellow-toothed maw as it neared, followed leisurely out of the darkness by the rest of the creature, apparently in no hurry. The beast was dark grey in color, the color of graphite, and looked to be nearly furless, just bare waxy skin on its long slender legs, with coarse greasy hairs sprouting here and there out of its massive shoulders. The sparse hairs thickened and toughened as they went up its hunched back, finally turning into a row of sharp spines as thick and long as a finger running all the way down its backbone.

The creature slowly approached the little group, seemingly stalking them, staring at them hungrily with its bulbous black eyes full of malice. "Wha…?" said Basher, taking another step back towards Shawn and Philo, not believing what he was seeing but knowing in an instant what the creature was and from what direction it had just come. "Chupacabra! ...Mother!" he cried, and lowering his head to give the creature the full force of his horns, Basher flung himself forward without a moment's hesitation.

The creature was slightly taken aback by the unexpected assault but focused its eyes on the humans, giving little attention to the goat and tossing Basher over its shoulder like a banana peel. With the humans in front of the creature, and the goat behind, Basher shouted "Run!" and took off, bleating in fear for his mother, in the direction of their chamber. Philo dropped the flashlight and he and Shawn wasted no time trying to retrieve it, instead turning rapidly on their heels and going back in the direction that they had come from.

"Run, Shawn, run!" shouted Philo. "We've got to get up high! Find a place where we can climb! We need to climb up something!" The beast was close behind them, picking up speed as it matched the boys in acceleration, but still taking its time, as if it realized that it had won the race as soon as it had begun. The teens were no match for the creature, having no weapons, neither claws nor teeth, neither bullets nor blades. Philo's thoughts suddenly went to a little pocket knife he carried and he reached in his cargo pants for it, knowing that it would be totally ineffectual against this creature.

His fingers found the object and he grasped it tightly, for comfort more than protection. Drawing it out of his pocket, he saw its steel case shine faintly in the darkness as he opened the largest of the blades. The blade locked open with a snap, the action causing Philo's nervous fingers to drop it. He heard it clatter against a stone on the path as he ran on, losing sight of it completely. With no possibility to stop and look for his lost pocketknife, Philo had to admit the futility of using the tiny two inch blade against the monster at their heels.

The creature's large black eyes were made for seeing in the dark and although it had fallen behind and didn't have a line of sight on the cousins, its long snout with its wet canine-like nose pinpointed their position and savored the smell of frightened terror emanating from the humans. From where they were around a bend in the tunnel some short distance ahead, Philo and Shawn continued to run as fast as they could into the darkness, feeling along the rock walls. Shawn called in a panic to his cousin. "These walls are too smooth! There's no where to climb!" Although they could not see it, they could still hear the creature's wet panting breath, full of saliva, and smell its rank greasy odor, knowing for certain that it was still there, that it was savoring the hunt and anticipating the reward of their slaughter. Seeing a mild glow, Shawn called to Philo, "Quick, take that turn ahead!" Going around the corner with the beast close behind, the cousins found themselves in a bad spot. Philo exclaimed to Shawn, "Oh no, a dead end!" Indeed, the passageway had led them into a small cave with no exit.

***

"Well, that certainly looks better," said Marsha, smiling not just at the cleaned up and packed up campsite, but also at the sight of her parents, laying together on the hood of the pickup truck, backs leaning against the windshield, talking quietly and enjoying the eventful day's end.

Trudy looked up at the sound of her daughter's voice and smiled. "Good job, you all. Looks like it's time to go... If those boys would get back. I wonder what's keeping them..."

"I'll go see. I feel rested enough. This fresh air and solstice sun light are making me feel human again! Hey, Gadget, whaddya say you help me find those kids... there's no use in me getting lost too!" Frank called to Candy. "Hey, girl, c'mon, help us find Shawn."

They headed back into the tunnel and after a hundred yards or so, Frank began hollering for the teens. "Sha-awn! Phi-lo! You wouldn't think it would take so long for them to get back out again. I still can't believe it about the gold! It's too funny that after all the people who have come over here searching for the lost gold of Ladron Peak that Shawn and Philo would succeed. Of course, the Ruminators had a hand in it too."

Candy had run ahead in the tunnel, romping back and forth, trying to get Gadget and Frank to chase her. She ran back to them, then ran on again, and was a hundred yards or so further in front of them when she stopped and listened, a familiar howling noise coming to her ears. From where Gadget and Frank stood, it sounded as though there was a coyote in the tunnel, but Candy knew that the creature making that sound was not just a local coyote who took a wrong turn. Candy crouched down as the fur along her spine stood upright. Her ears were also at attention, focused on the tunnel ahead as she briefly bared her teeth and emitted a low growl. Then raising her muzzle to the tunnel's ceiling, she howled a reply, a warning to the creature to stay away.

Frank called after Candy, alarmed at the sound of a coyote howling in the tunnel and suddenly alarmed at the idea of Shawn and Philo coming into contact with it. Frank's body was facing exhaustion after an entire day on the run, and his mind wasn't faring any better. Returning to his happy laughing family had caused a schism in his brain as it tried to reconcile the present with the past. Frank's neurons were firing rapidly, hearing the beast down here in the tunnel while standing next to Gadget, but his receptors were having none of it, and Frank found that he couldn't think clearly. He only thought that at worst, the present danger would be in the form of a trapped coyote. Frightening enough for a mind that didn't dare contemplate any alternatives, such as having those he loved come into contact with a hideous monster. Especially the one engineered by General Schwinger's laboratory. "Candy!" he called. "Get away! Come on good dog!"

Candy ignored her master's orders and charged ahead down the tunnel, finding, as she knew she would, the second of the creatures that the soldiers had released. Candy had met a chupacabra before and had beaten it. It had been the creature that Frank had seen in their own yard all those months back. She had encountered the thing as it had skulked around the chicken coop and she had chased it down into the bosque and had bitten and shaken it, over and over, until it was dead. But Candy was mistaken. This creature that she was about to engage with was not the same as the one that she had killed.

That creature, killed by her that night long ago in the bosque, was the chupacabra of local legend, created by simple mutation, and it was terrible enough, but this thing in the tunnel was a monster. A product of an evil engineering program that radiated it and tinkered with its DNA to target and hone its mindlessly superior killing skills. This was one of Schwinger's mutant army and Candy was about to meet it, unaware.

Candy held nothing back as she came upon the beast and she flew at the creature with all she had. The beast was not surprised, its senses of sight and smell, better than Candy's, knew that the dog was coming, but it was surprised by the yellow dog's power and strength. Candy went straight for its throat, not wanting to play around, but the creature was ready for her, turning its neck so that Candy received the sharp spikes of the creature's back instead of its soft throat. One spine pierced Candy's cheek and tore out again, and she howled in pain, flinging herself once more at the creature, aiming again for its neck. The blow knocked the creature backward and it stumbled for a moment.

Candy took advantage of the tumble and she lunged again, this time her teeth made purchase into one of the creature's big black eyes. The beast howled in pain, snarling and snapping as it groped around with its jaws for its canine assailant. The creature's bites were narrowly missing her, and Candy realized that she had managed to blind it somewhat, giving her an excellent advantage. She targeted its throat again, but missed as the creature thrashed about, once again slicing Candy across the shoulder with its spines. Candy snapped again, aiming this time for the creatures eyes, one of which was already a painful open wound. As her teeth sank into the other of the creature's big black eyes, she held on to its head with her strong jaws, kicking it repeatedly in its soft underbelly with her back legs. The creature wriggled free of Candy's bite and flailed around, the spines on its back opening another nasty gash, this time across Candy's ribs.

Back up the tunnel, Frank and Gadget could hear the fight and instinctively began to run towards it, to help the dog, to stop the fight. Gadget called out to Frank that they needed a weapon of some sort. "We can't possibly fight Schwinger's monster with our bare hands!" she hollered.

A light went on in Frank's head that filled him with horror. Instantly the image of the coyote he had held in his mind was replaced with an image of the creature, the mutant chupacabra, and he shouted in anguish. "Oh no!" he cried, "That beast! The boys! Candy! What can we do?" He reached down and picked up a handful of rocks, instantly making himself feel foolish and ineffectual, like the story of David and Goliath, but worse of course, because this wasn't just a story. How could there possibly be the slaying of a giant with a few small stones? How could they possibly defeat the monster with a handful of pebbles? "Candy! Hang on, we're coming!" declared Frank, charging ahead anyway.

Back down the tunnel, the creature hadn't lost an ounce of its energy, but its blindness and anger were causing it to attack wildly, its ability to effectively target its attacks lost. More and more, the beast was leaving itself open to Candy's counterattacks. Candy was in a froth of fury and pain, and nearing exhaustion. The beast snapped at her blindly with its powerful jaws, still landing enough of the bites to wear her down and it managed to tear off a large chunk of Candy's left ear which caused the yellow dog to fly backwards. Candy was struggling to right herself, twisting on her back, when the creature leapt on top of her. Suddenly, from back up the tunnel, a sound came to Candy's torn and bloodied ears, the reassuring sound of Frank's voice, telling her that he was nearby.

Hearing Frank's voice reignited Candy's desire to protect those she loved and those she had grown to love with everything she had and the dog regained some of her energy. She did not falter, but instantly lunged with her jaws, again and again from her position on the ground while the blinded creature, fueled by

216

nothing that was good, snapped down at her from its position on her tender belly. The creature loomed over her, and though it could not see her, it could smell the very blood coursing powerfully through her veins. The creature parted its sharp teeth and made a move for her neck while exposing his own soft throat at the same time.

In the dimness, Gadget and Frank came upon the horrible scene and Gadget looked at Frank, her face full of confusion and horror. The sounds in the darkness had been terrible! Cries of canine anger, pain and agony, combined with the sounds of a wild animal, tortured and torturing, until finally there was no sound at all. Gadget raised her tiny lantern, illuminating the bodies of the two torn and bloody creatures lying in the path.

***

The chamber Philo and Shawn found themselves in was indeed brighter than the dark passageway, and the boys squinted, eyes more accustomed to the near blackness of the tunnels since the loss of the flashlight, and they scanned the cave walls for any kind of exit. Confirming that there was indeed no way out, they began to look for a way up, and they searched higher up the walls. No handholds, no footholds, just smooth granite all around. In fact, the only indent that the boys could see in the rock was the small gap, high overhead, that was letting in a shaft of light. No way they could reach it. The longest day of the year was ending and the final rays of solstice sunlight were there to greet the horrible scene that was about to unfold. As the setting sun moved over and behind the mountain, the shaft of light increased in color and intensity and bathed the cave in a blood red glow.

Philo whispered urgently to Shawn, "Get behind me, I'll find something to hit it with!" Looking on the floor and finding no loose stones or rocks, he suddenly remembered the water bottle bag hanging from his shoulder and took out the gold bar. They could hear the creature approaching, its wet rattling wheeze echoing louder and louder in the tunnel as it neared. From far away the cousins heard the sound of a howl as though a coyote in pain was trapped in a well. The beast just outside the chamber heard it too and paused momentarily, listening as its partner fought with the dog Candy. But this beast had more pressing business to attend to, and was not particularly interested in being social or cooperative with its own kind. The creature turned once again toward the chamber and lowered its body, preparing to engage with the teens. As the beast entered into the little cave, Philo backed further into the corner pushing Shawn behind him. He grasped the gold brick in both hands and raised it over his head, ready to throw it at the creature. The beast slunk towards them, big black eyes squinting to narrow slits at the red setting sunlight filling the space.

Shawn shifted slightly behind his cousin, trying to wriggle one of the bricks out of his own bag as he whispered to Philo, "Nice knowing you, I guess this dead end makes us even for the fool's gold fiasco." The comment caused the creature to snarl, though it seemed to be having some difficulty with its eyes. The creature actually seemed to be experiencing pain from the light.

Philo still had the gold bar raised above his head as Shawn yelled, "Throw it!" Philo was preparing to propel the bar forward when the shaft of light hit the brick and bounced off, changing the color in the chamber from blood red to a warm golden hue. This last shaft of the setting solstice sunlight then hit the creature squarely in its hungry black eyes and it stumbled for a moment, blinded. The creature's pain soon became obvious, and the beast contorted its greasy body back toward the wall of the cave. Shawn exclaimed, "The light, it doesn't like the light!" as he finally managed to get one of the gold bars out of the bag that he had slung around his body and he held it up, trying to find the right angle to train another beam of light onto the beast. With two shafts of solstice light shining into the face of creature, it let out a rattling scream, the sound of an animal in supreme agony.

Then a very strange thing began to happen. The beast snarled and snapped as its whole posture began to change. Its hunched backbone began to straighten, causing the creature to arch its back and it let out a chilling howl. The creature seemed to shrink before their eyes, its overall size began to decrease, as the muscles of the beast's massive shoulders seemed to shrivel instantaneously. Shawn and Philo watched in awe, still carefully keeping the shafts of fading light shining directly onto the creature. The beast continued to writhe around on the cave floor and the spines that had protruded along its back softened into long thick guard hairs while the rest of the creature's sparse greasy fur began to soften. A pelt of smooth and glossy hairs began to sprout, light brown and black, all over its body, covering the sickly grey skin. The eyes of the creature, the previously hungry bulbous black eyes, clouded over, still showing pain, but now adding an expression of fear as well, and the creature shut them tight. When next they blinked open, the eyes were much smaller and softer looking. No longer did they have the look of an alien life form, they had changed to a beautiful golden brown color. At last the creature let out a small whimpering cry and lay on the floor, looking like nothing more than an exhausted coyote.

Epilogue

Frank was siting on a folding chair in front of a blanket spread on the ground. There were several coolers around, each one stocked full of all manner of fruits and veggies, both exotic and domestic. Frank paused to smile at his friends. All of the Ruminators had turned out for the picnic, everyone above ground and enjoying the warm sunshine. Several of the Ruminators were trying on sandals from a big bin of them provided by Frank and his family and Nougat and Nugget were arguing good-naturedly over a pair of pink flip-flops. Salizar was lying on the blanket, stroking the fur of a young black and white border collie. "Where will you go now?" Frank asked. "You know, you are all welcome to stay around here. I know there's not much water and the browsing is pretty slim pickings, but Marsha won't mind making runs to the produce market now that she has her license!"

Marsha smiled at her father, and mouthed the words, "thank you," referring to the cute yellow pickup truck she now owned that was parked on the dirt road just down the hill. Marsha had angled for a sports car since her dad stood to make a lot of money from the book and movie rights to their story, but he had said, "No dice, a dirt road is a dirt road, and I'm sure not going to be making enough money to get ours paved. A sports car would get destroyed in no time!" Shawn had angled for a sports car too, even though a license for him was more than a year away. He even jokingly threatened to use one of the gold bars to buy one, but Trudy was firm. The gold bars were just going to be pretty doorstops until it was time to pay for college. For once, Shawn didn't roll his eyes, and in the meantime got a nifty little ATV to tool around on, and another one for Philo to use when he visited.

Salizar smiled warmly at Frank and his offer to remain in Bernardo. "No, we must go. It seems as though we have resigned ourselves to staying hidden. But with our new friend Whisper here and without that false chupacabra around, at least we will no longer be on the run," she said, continuing to pet the collie. "We will be forever grateful, my friends."

Frank put a hand over his eyes to shade them and looked up at the mountain. "Funny that those big black alien-looking eyes that were so good for locating prey in the dark, turned out to be their weakest attribute."

Basher took a sip from his new water bottle, the one that Philo had given him that day down in the tunnel and he smiled at his mother. "I sure am glad things turned out as they did," he said, putting his hand to her shoulder. Sage of course agreed, proud of her son and glad that she hadn't been home on the day that the chupacabra came to call. "Candy sure did show herself to be a major protector didn't she? How's she doing?"

"She's healing well from the ordeal. ...Got her in a huge soft beanbag chair in Shawn's room. Biggest and fluffiest we could find. Put it right underneath the swamp cooler vent. The vet says there won't be any permanent damage, other than the cosmetic damage to her ear and a few nasty scars. She should be back to her old cuddly lazy self soon." Frank couldn't help but ask Salizar one more time for the Ruminators to stick around. "We really would love to have you stay with us. It's private, and we'd never let on about your existence unless you wanted us to," said Frank.

Frank had told his story to the press, leaving out the parts about the strange herd of goats that were camped under Ladron Peak, and Sergeant Wilson had backed him up on the story. It looked like General Schwinger, the crazy maverick evil nut case, was going to get his due in rapid fashion. It was all a big embarrassment for the government, that they hadn't kept a close eye on this small but expensive research facility, and the place had been shut down instantly. As a bonus, all of the high tech equipment from the big beige building was promised to the Albuquerque Biopark to assist their breeding programs in saving endangered species. To Frank's dismay, all of the creatures had to be destroyed. They had tried to turn them back to regular coyotes, like Shawn and Philo had done down in the cave, but the circumstances couldn't be recreated. Something to do with the solstice and the gold and, well, nobody knew. Gadget shifted uneasily behind Salizar. She was enjoying the picnic enormously, but she had grown very fond of Frank and the rest of his family and was not ready to leave her new friends. Salizar glanced over her shoulder at her and smiled. "Of course," Salizar said, "we would like to take advantage of your offer... in one small way..."

"Anything," said Trudy, sitting in a folding chair next to Frank, her arm entwined in his. "Anything at all, Salizar. We have loved getting to know the Ruminators; we have loved the adventure, the friendship, and the remarkable education of it all..."

"Interestingly enough, bleat, that's just what I want to ask you about - education. If we Ruminators are going to survive along side of the human race, but hidden from it, we shall need more knowledge. Knowledge about humans, knowledge about the world... So it is with your permission, and your generous offer, that I make a request on behalf of our herd. We ask that our friend Gidget here, sorry, Gadget I mean, remain with you for a time. At your house across the river. Until she learns to read.

We would like her to bring this skill to our entire herd." Salizar paused and looked at Gadget's hopeful face. "In due time, of course... when she is proficient."

Frank knelt down next to the little white goat and produced a well worn paperback book from his back pocket. Holding it up, Frank said happily, "Reading lessons for Gadget? With pleasure!"

The End

THE LINGERLINGS

Dr. Frank Mater, Ph.D., has a reputation for being somewhat of a cryptid expert, owing to his strange experience with a nasty pair of chupacabras. So when he hears that someone has reported seeing an unusual creature in the forests of east Texas, the zoologist enlists his kids and their cousin to go and check it out. Just for fun.

Last summer, Marsha, Shawn, and Philo had an unbelievable adventure in (and under) the New Mexico desert. They aren't expecting a repeat of that kind of excitement on this camping trip with Dad, but when the young explorers finally catch up with the odd little animal, they find more than just a suspected living fossil.

Is this strange creature a remnant of Earth's past that has somehow remained hidden from the progression of time, or could it actually be an otherworldly piece of our Universe's future?

THE LINGERLINGS, sequel to THE RUMINATORS, is a sci-fi adventure for YA audiences that is full of environmental consciousness, interesting facts, and strange fantasies about our world and who just might be visiting us.